WHEN A CAT LOVES A DOG

MARY E. LOWD

For Daniel

CONTENTS

CHAPTER 1

The pug dogs in the pews couldn't help snickering at the sight of a black cat in a white wedding dress. Lashonda knew they were laughing at her, but she strained to keep her ears pointed forward as she walked alone down the aisle. She couldn't let anything break her composure, not with so many eyes on her. She had to make it through the ceremony without losing her dignity.

At least Topher's family had come to the wedding. Lashonda's parents and all but one of her sisters had refused. They didn't want to see her marry a dog. The few cats who had come looked mighty uncomfortable sitting in the pews surrounded by Topher's pug relatives and other canine friends. Unlike most cats, Lashonda didn't mind being surrounded by dogs, but it stung that her family was so poorly represented at her own wedding. It didn't help that she felt all the canine eyes in the room judging her and finding her humorous. She'd told Topher they should elope.

Lashonda gripped her bouquet tighter, digging her claws into the fabric wrapped base of the white dogwood blossoms and silver sprigs of pussy willow. Why couldn't their families get along as peacefully as her symbolic flowers?

Lashonda reached the end of the aisle and was relieved to have the audience finally behind her. She could still hear their laughter and feel their eyes on her, but she didn't have to see them anymore. She saw only Topher.

Topher held out a tawny-furred paw to her, and she took it as she stepped up onto the dais beside him. He leaned close and whispered, "I should have written a few jokes for the preacher to read, since my family can't seem to help laughing. Can't blame 'em, though: I do look funny in a tux."

The muscles around Lashonda's ears relaxed, and her green eyes smiled at him. She knew it wasn't true that his family was laughing at *him*, but she let Topher's words shield her anyway. Topher handled the spotlight with such grace. Of course, he had practice. He was a stand-up comedian.

Every time Lashonda had been to one of Topher's shows, she'd felt nervous for him, watching him up on the stage. Now she was onstage beside him. When Lashonda had watched Topher perform at night clubs, she always heard the words of his jokes echo in her mind a moment before he said them, as if she were prompting him, helping him to remember. Not that Topher needed help. She'd never seen him nervous, except for when he'd asked her to marry him.

Lashonda imagined that Topher was onstage in a night club now. This was one of his routines, and all she had to do was follow along. Her emerald eyes locked onto his brown ones. The joyful, goofy grin that transformed his jowly muzzle was almost enough to block Lashonda's ears to the quiet chortling from the rest of the church. She squeezed his paw tight, and Topher's blunt claws clicked together; she carefully kept her own razor sharp claws sheathed to keep from piercing his paw pads.

The preacher, a Jellicle cat, cleared his throat. He was the only preacher they'd found who was willing to perform a mixed-species wedding ceremony. Lashonda broke her gaze away from Topher, and they both turned to face the Jellicle preacher.

Standing in front of the multi-colorful, many faceted stained glass window that rose up behind the dais, Lashonda and the preacher cut striking figures. Lashonda's midnight fur contrasted starkly with her dress, and the preacher's black and white splotches matched his formal suit beautifully. The monochromatic lines of their bodies held all the poise and elegance of any feline.

In comparison, Topher did look funny. The wrinkled folds of his snub-nosed muzzle always looked silly; his short tank-like, barrel-chested stature was hard to take seriously in a double-breasted tux with bowtie and tails. He was a natural clown, and only another dog—or a cat in love—could see him as handsome. Almost everyone in the church, cats and dogs alike, was thinking how the bride looked better matched to the preacher than her groom. Everyone except Lashonda. The thought didn't even cross her mind.

The Jellicle preacher read to the room from a prayer book with gilt-edged pages. He spoke about love and harmony, opposites attracting, and commitment in the face of adversity. While he spoke, Lashonda lost herself in his words and in Topher's eyes. For a while the rest of the church went away.

When he led Topher and Lashonda through the traditional vows, Lashonda marveled that her tongue didn't trip up over the words, embarrassing her. Completely unexpectedly, Topher's voice broke over his vows. He never fumbled the words to his jokes! Lashonda treasured the sincere show of emotion that could make her Topher, a hardened veteran of the stage, stumble over the words in a few simple vows.

As they exchanged rings, whispered woofs in the pews broke Lashonda's concentration. Her ears flicked, trying to listen and trying not to listen at the same time. All of her focus should be on Topher and the moment they were sharing. She could worry about dealing with his family later. Let them think what they liked; they couldn't change what was happening. Lashonda was Topher's family now, and only he had any say in that.

The preacher took a paw from each of them and held their paws up high in the air. Lashonda felt a rising sense of excitement as the preacher announced, "I now have the honor of introducing to you: Westopher and Lashonda Brooke, husband and wife!"

The preacher brought their paws together and invited them to kiss. Their muzzles met, whiskers intermingling electrically, in a kiss that rivaled their first. The church fell silent.

Topher and Lashonda walked back down the aisle together. Topher's corkscrew of a tail wagged furiously behind his tux, and Lashonda's tail strained under the heavy skirts of her bouffant gown, trying to stand tall.

The dogs of various breeds who were Topher's night club and comedian friends barked cheerily, sounding happy for the newlywed couple as they walked by. The faces of Lashonda's sister and feline friends from the engineering lab were harder to read—*polite, appropriate, but baffled*, Lashonda thought. The eyes of Topher's family burned into her.

Outside the church's main sanctuary, the Jellicle preacher joined the newlyweds, having taken the side door out to meet them. He directed them into a small room with a table where all their paperwork was laid out. "I know I said you were married before. But I lied. It won't be official until you sign all of these."

Lashonda could hear the guests moving around outside in the church's main lobby now. One of Topher's friends, an Afghan Hound night club owner, had been solicited to direct the guests into the church's fellowship hall for the reception. All Topher and Lashonda had been able to afford was snacks, cake, and beverages in the church. Nonetheless, Lashonda knew that the cake was a traditional three-tiered confection, frosted with a pale pink salmon mousse; each table was graced with a cut-glass bowl full of bacon candies; and the heavy cream would flow freely. For a small scale affair, it would be lavish.

But first the paperwork.

Lashonda's sister Kelly, a tortoiseshell tabby, slipped away from the crowd and joined the newlyweds. She had agreed to be their witness for the paperwork.

The Jellicle preacher offered pens to all three of them—bride, groom, and witness. "I had to alter the forms a little," he said. With an extended claw, he pointed at a pair of checkboxes near the top of the marriage license—it offered two options: canine and feline. "There wasn't a premade form for a mixed marriage. So, I simply wrote *groom* over the canine box, and *bride* over feline. I checked with preachers who've done this in other counties. It should be fine."

The Jellicle preacher's tone was airy, as if this were a minor inconvenience. However, the slight stung Lashonda. Being with Topher felt like the most natural thing in the world to her, but everyone and everything else resisted their union. Finally out of the spotlight, without the eyes of all their friends and family turned her way, Lashonda was free to experience her feelings without repressing and filtering them. Her ears flattened, tight against her skull.

A bark broke out behind them, "What is this?"

Lashonda turned to see her new mother-in-law, Gladiola, standing in the doorway, resplendent in a pink pants-suit and wide-brimmed hat decorated with netting and faux flowers. Her goofy, pug face was distorted by shock and horror.

"We're signing the papers, Ma," Topher said. "The reception's across the hall. We'll be there in a minute." He turned back to the table and signed his name with a flourish.

Kelly followed his lead, signing her name with a little less panache on the *witness* line. "How hard could it be to print up a few new forms after the laws changed?" she grumbled, giving voice to her sister's irritation.

The Jellicle preacher slid the forms on the table toward Lashonda. She lowered her pen to the paper; her claws extended, curving around it, as she signed her new name, *Lashonda Brooke*, for the first time.

The Jellicle preacher's whiskers spread in a smile, and he said, "There, now you're really husband and wife. Go enjoy your reception!"

Topher wrapped his arms around Lashonda's waist, and she leaned her head against him, rubbing the fur on the side of her face against the folds of his jowls.

"You mean," Gladiola said, "this was a real wedding?"

"What did you think it was?" Kelly asked scornfully.

"One of Topher's comedy things." Gladiola looked at her son, wrapped lovingly around his feline bride. "You're always pulling stunts and putting on skits. Remember those magic shows you put on for the other puppies when you wanted to be a magician?" The pleading edge of a whine entered her voice. "This is a joke, right? You can't have a real marriage with a cat."

Kelly spat and muttered imprecations under her breath.

Lashonda's curiosity moved her tongue, and she asked, "Why the hell not?" Simultaneously, Topher said the words that should have ended it all: "Indeed I can."

Gladiola answered her new daughter-in-law's question with a matter-of-fact simplicity that ignored all the love and affection in her son's eyes, not to mention years of rising political tension and legal upheaval in the realm of feline rights: "You can't give him puppies."

"We don't want children," Lashonda said. The words came easily. She'd practiced them many times with her parents. She'd had her doubts about motherhood since she was a kitten herself, and she could hardly have spent the last two years dating a dog without the subject coming up. "We've talked about it."

When Lashonda brought Topher home to meet her family, it was the first time her sisters had really believed she never intended to have kittens. Adelle and Sherri still hadn't forgiven her for shattering their dreams of picnics in the park with all of their litters—a dozen hypothetical cousin-kittens—playing together. Kelly, however, had promised that Lashonda could be her kittens' favorite aunt when she had them.

"Is this true?" Gladiola asked Topher.

"No, Ma," Topher said, completely deadpan. "I've never discussed child-rearing with this cat. In fact, I didn't even know she was a cat." His eyes took on a hysterical light. "Help! Help! I've married the wrong person!"

Gladiola glared at her son. "This is serious."

Topher leveled his gaze at his mother and said, "I know. When I'm willing to make a joke out of something, it shows I'm serious. And there's nothing I'm more serious about than Lashonda. Now, back off."

Gladiola's expression bespoke shock. "But you've always wanted to be a father!" she blurted. "You've wanted to be a father since you were a little puppy! How could you possibly be happy with a cat who can't give you a litter?"

"I will be happy," Topher said, his jowls firmly set. "That's all you need to know. Now, please, *leave*."

Kelly stepped between the two pug dogs and took Gladiola by the arm. "Come on," she said. "Come with me, and we'll go over to the reception. It's right across the way in the Fellowship Hall. I'm sure Topher and Lashonda will join us soon." Kelly purred soothing words at Gladiola, telling her all about the salmon mousse cake and bacon candies as she firmly guided her out of the room.

"I'm so sorry," Topher said. "I didn't know she thought... I mean..." Topher didn't want to use the word *joke* to describe their wedding, even in referring to someone else's thoughts. He frowned. "I guess this explains the pug lady that Ma kept trying to introduce me to before the ceremony."

Lashonda remembered seeing a pug woman she didn't recognize with Topher's family. She'd looked to be about her and Topher's age, and she was wearing a splashy, off-the-shoulder red dress. It was a date night dress. Most definitely. Lashonda had wondered who she was.

Topher covered his face with his paws. "I can't believe my mother brought a date for me to my own wedding."

Lashonda flattened her ears. "You're kidding, right?"

The Jellicle preacher snickered.

"I wish I was," Topher said, face still hidden behind his paws.

The Jellicle preacher cleared his throat and said, "For what it's worth, I've seen a lot worse."

Lashonda raised her ears, curious.

"Yeah?" Topher said, peering from between his claws. "Tell us about it."

"The first mixed-species marriage I officiated was in Old York right after the laws changed." The Jellicle preacher gathered up the marriage license papers, separated them out into two copies, and slipped one set into a manila envelope as he spoke. "The bride was the smallest Chihuahua woman I've ever seen and the groom was this big, beefy tomcat with orange stripes. The Chihuahua was some sort of hotel baron's daughter. A bit of a celebrity, I guess." He slipped the second marriage license into a fancy folder with a satin finish and handed it to Lashonda. "She wore a *pink* wedding dress." He shook his head. "Anyway, halfway through the ceremony, cops showed up to arrest the groom. I rushed through the vows while they read him his rights, and they slapped the cuffs on him while he was saying 'I do.' Then they dragged him off to spend the night in jail."

Lashonda pictured the orange tom trying to exchange rings with his bride while handcuffed. It was a sad picture. "I thought you said this was after the laws changed. Why did they arrest him?"

"Apparently the bride's father was so upset about his daughter marrying a cat that he called the police and said she'd been kidnapped, that a crazy tomcat was blackmailing her into marrying him against her will."

"And it took all night to get it sorted out?" Lashonda asked, wide-eyed.

The Jellicle preacher nodded.

"That's a lousy way to spend your wedding night," Topher said.

"I told you I'd seen worse. Make you feel better?"

"A bit," Topher admitted.

Lashonda traced a claw around the edge of her precious marriage license. She was glad that dogs and cats like the Chihuahua and the handcuffed tom had blazed the way, making it easier for her and Topher. The fur along her spine prickled against the silk of her gown to think that she and Topher were really married.

"Come on," she said. "There's a salmon mousse cake waiting for us to cut it." A wicked glint entered Lashonda's eye: "Also, I hear, a pug lady waiting to be disappointed."

Topher harrumphed. "I'll be disappointing all the ladies from now on, except for you." He turned to the Jellicle preacher and looked him up and down, sizing him up. "You know, if you wanted to try this mixed marriage thing out for yourself, I think I know a single pug girl who my mother could set you up with."

The Jellicle preacher looked stricken. He turned to Lashonda and said, "He's joking now? Right?"

"Right," Lashonda said. If Topher's mother thought the pug in the red dress was a suitable match for her son, then that pug lady was probably expecting a husband who could give her perfect, wrinkle-faced pug puppies. A Jellicle tomcat wouldn't work at all.

Lashonda sneered inside at Gladiola's idea of a "real marriage." It was so limited. Though, as she thought it, she remembered what Gladiola had said about Topher always wanting to be a father, ever since he'd been a puppy. That couldn't be true. It wasn't what Topher had told her. Had he been hiding his real feelings from her?

Kelly poked her head back into the little room, ears skewed, and said, "Aren't you guys done yet? There's a whole room full of cats and dogs trying to be polite to each other while they wait for you."

"That shouldn't be hard," Lashonda said through gritted teeth.

"Shouldn't," Kelly said. "But it is. It's the truth of the world. If you want to get away from it, go live on an otter space station."

Topher and Lashonda exchanged a glance. Lashonda wanted to ask Topher about his mother's words, but it wasn't the time. There was a three-tiered cake to cut, toasts to be made with fluted glasses of frothy cream, and congratulations—some sincere, some less so—to receive. Lashonda reached out a paw to her new husband. As their paw pads intertwined, she felt the smooth band of his wedding ring sitting snuggly in the fur at the base of his finger. Whatever Gladiola said or knew about Topher, that ring was a promise that he was hers now. She would take care of him. She would make him happy, whatever it took.

Kelly led her sister and new brother-in-law across the church to their reception.

CHAPTER 2

Topher and Lashonda had wanted to spend their honeymoon on the otter space station—spend a few days at Moonville Funpark, experiment with the oceanic cuisine, and look down at their world from thousands of kilometers in the air. Topher thought it would be the ultimate romantic getaway, but Lashonda insisted that anywhere they went would be romantic. Their honeymoon could feel like heaven without literally taking place in the heavens.

Besides, tickets up the space elevator were expensive, and they needed to save their money for rent and tuition until she finished graduate school and was hired by an engineering lab or he picked up a more stable gig. As it was, they combined their honeymoon with a stand-up tour for Topher. They traveled down the coast, staying in a different town every night.

During the days, they explored the towns together. Despite their variations, each town seemed to hold at least one sweets shop, and Topher made a point of trying the peanut butter fudge in every town. Lashonda discovered a love for the kite shops. Their displays mesmerized her: colorful kites, pinwheels, and windsocks out front fluttered and dipped in the windy coastal weather. Lashonda imagined flying like the kites did. Her eyes followed their strings up into the sky, and her heart followed.

Every evening, they hit the local gin joint for a greasy dinner—it wasn't otter cuisine, but it was still seafood. After dinner, Topher took to the stage to deliver his stand-up routine while Lashonda listened with one ear to the jokes she'd heard dozens of times before. She still enjoyed hearing them, but she saved the other half of her attention for working on her thesis. She typed away at her beat-up, old, second-hand laptop computer, polishing the massive document that described the experiments she'd been running on synthesis of hardened plastic via laser activation of powdered polymers. The specifics were technical, but the vision was simple: Lashonda was trying to build a machine that could print three-dimensional objects from blueprints fed to it by a computer.

On the last day, Topher and Lashonda passed another kite shop while strolling through the final village. Lashonda stopped to stare at the kites shaped like butterflies and bumble-bees, spaceships and silver-scaled fish, all tied to the driftwood railing in front of the shop and whizzing in the wind.

"You should buy one," Topher said.

Lashonda skewed one ear to the side skeptically. "Why would I need a kite?"

"Oh, come on. You get that look in your eyes every time we walk past one of these shops. That look that says, *I want to own the thing I'm looking at, possess it for myself.*" Topher looked smug. "It's the same look you started to give me not long before I proposed."

Lashonda twisted her ears to the side to hide the sudden pink inside them that would give away her blush. She looked at the kites flying out front of the shop and tried to imagine owning one of them.

"It's also the same look you give the last fried clam in every basket of clams we order," Topher said.

"Is that why you always give me the last one?"

Topher snorted. "Of course. Now pick out a kite, and let's go fly it on the beach."

Lashonda spent an hour inside the shop, examining every kite they had. It gave her an extra zip of excitement to know that one of them would leave the store with her. Topher was right: she did want to own one.

Finally, she settled on the first kite that had caught her eye —one of the long, thin fish with glittering silver scales. She wanted to see it shine in the sun. They took their purchase out of the shop and down the winding concrete stairs from the lane of tourist emporiums to the beach.

The sun glared hotly, and wind swept the tufts of beach grass. It was a perfect day for flying kites. There were several other kites already in the air, brightening up the blue sky, and Lashonda recognized a few of them as twins to the ones she'd seen in the kite shop. Most of them, though, looked homemade —simple diamonds in different solid colors, built over a cross and trailing simple tails of streamers.

When Lashonda's fish kite hit the wind, it took to the sky like a real fish released back into water. Its scales twinkled, dancing and undulating as the wind currents gave it life, and its dark eyes winked down at her. It bucked against the string, held tightly in Lashonda's paws, trying to escape and fly freely into the giant ocean of sky.

Lashonda couldn't help but laugh. She felt like a giant space cat, hind paws on Earth but front paws reaching up to fish the sky for interstellar ichthyoids.

Lashonda turned to Topher to offer him a chance holding the string, but he'd wandered off. She twisted her ears around, listening for a hint of his deep voice, but the wind stole any traces of his voice as surely as it confused the feeling in her whiskers.

She narrowed her eyes against the glare of sun, bright in the sky and reflecting off the surf and sand, to look more closely at the other groups dotting the beach nearest to her. North along the sand, a pair of collies leaned against each other on a romantic walk. A Dalmatian jogged along the edge of the surf. A Siamese cat wrangled a bumblebee shaped kite against the wind. Further in the distance, several larger groups picnicked on blankets stretched out on the sand.

Lashonda looked south and saw a group of puppies, terrier mixes, huddled over a patch of blue on the beach. She needed look no further: Topher crouched beside them, moving his paws over the patch of blue. Squinting harder, Lashonda realized it was a blue diamond kite, and Topher held its string— either tying or untangling it. When he finished, Topher held the blue diamond up. The puppies jumped up and down, clapping their paws. One of the puppies, dressed in a yellow sundress, threw her paws around Topher's waist. Topher had fixed her kite for her.

Lashonda watched Topher help the puppy in the yellow sundress get her kite flying again. He ran along the beach beside her until her blue diamond took to the sky. The other puppies ran after them, launching their own diamonds of color into the sky beside hers. Topher slowed, and all the puppies ran on down the beach past him. He stood watching them for a while, then he turned and saw Lashonda watching him. He grinned and held out his arms like a weight-lifter. Lashonda could see that he felt like a hero.

He looked like a proud father.

Lashonda had never seen him that way before. She'd seen him in many lights—stage lights as the ambitious performer; harsh hospital lights when she broke her paw and he spent hours in waiting rooms and doctors' offices beside her; and the hazy, rosy lights of her imagination as she pictured him growing old with her. She'd never pictured him as a father.

Gladiola's words came back to her, *"You've always wanted to be a father!"*, and Lashonda wondered whether the fact that she'd never pictured Topher as a father before said more about her own desires than Topher's.

That night after dinner, Topher did his standard routine for the crowd at the Clam Dive Bar & Grill, but Lashonda couldn't concentrate on editing her thesis. The page of dry academic text glowed on the laptop screen before her eyes, but she didn't see it. Her vision was filled with imaginary puppies—little pug dogs like her Topher—listening raptly and laughing uproariously as Topher told silly, grade school jokes to them. She imagined them playing on the beach, tussling in a backyard, and being tucked into bed by their doting father.

Then she imagined herself with them. A whole litter of puppies nuzzled her, looked at her with those soulful brown eyes, and called her... mother. She'd never wanted to be a mama cat, but it was different when she imagined being mama to a litter of little Tophers.

Or maybe just one? Obviously, she and Topher couldn't have a litter of their own, but maybe they could adopt a puppy some day.

When Topher finished his routine, he worked his way around the room, shaking paws and accepting compliments. He checked in with the bartender, a mutt with a splotch over one eye who handed him his pay and introduced him to a Boston terrier dressed in suit and tie. The formal outfit stood out in a greasy spoon like the Clam Dive Bar & Grill.

Topher and the terrier talked together for quite a while. The rest of the patrons left, table by table, until Lashonda felt conspicuous sitting in a quiet restaurant with her beat up old laptop and mostly empty basket of shrimpy puffs.

Finally, she saw the Boston terrier hand Topher a card, shake his paw, and leave. Lashonda folded up her laptop and slipped it in its carrying case, readying herself to leave as well. Topher met her at the door.

They stepped outside into the chilly coastal evening, and Lashonda asked, "What was that about?"

Topher looked dazed. It took him a few moments to find the words. "That was a talent scout from The Nightly Howl."

Lashonda's heart skipped, tripped, and tumbled. The Nightly Howl was the biggest comedy/news show on the air. "*You're kidding*. Out here?"

Topher took Lashonda's laptop carrying case from her and slung it over his shoulder. He offered her a paw, and they started walking together, down toward the beach. The lights of the village hung ghostly in the mist that blew in off the sea. The beach was all sound, smell, and darkness—cold sand under foot pads; salt in the whiskers; and the rush, ebb, and flow of waves.

Topher's voice broke against the sound of the waves: "He said he has a friend a couple of towns back who saw my act and gave him a call. He knew I was working my way along the coast, so he flew out to see me."

Lashonda whispered the word, "Wow." An unvoiced whisper was all she could manage. Topher probably felt similarly overcome. At least, Lashonda assumed so. He wasn't saying anything.

They walked together for miles into the night, only turning back when the beach gave way to an impassable rocky outcropping. During daylight, they might have tried climbing it; or perhaps a path would have been visible. In the misty night, they turned back without a word.

Lashonda wanted to know everything the talent scout had said to Topher, but she was afraid to ask. If it wasn't good, she didn't want make Topher relive it. If it was good, she didn't want to get his hopes up. If it had been amazingly good, he'd have already told her.

"The Nightly Howl is even carried on some otter channels," Topher said, finally. "They watch it up on the space station."

"What did he say to you?" Lashonda asked, unable to contain her catly curiosity any longer.

"He said he'd call me." Topher's voice shook.

Lashonda's brave pug dog husband who only ever sounded nervous when he had asked her to marry him sounded petrified. She squeezed his paw, relishing in the feel of his strong, blunt claws against her fur.

There was no way to make the talent scout call sooner. All Lashonda could do was distract Topher, so she decided it was time to talk about the thoughts she'd had earlier that night. "At our wedding, your mom said you always wanted to be a father when you were a puppy."

Topher turned to her, and, in the diffuse light from the village up ahead, Lashonda saw the glint of surprise in his eyes. "Yeah," he said. "I used to steal the empty milk jugs from the recycling and draw faces on them. I made myself a whole litter before Pa relented and bought me a puppy-doll. He didn't think a litter of boys needed dolls to play with. He's kind of rigid. I'm surprised he didn't mind us getting married, but I guess he's more into gender stereotypes than breedism."

Lashonda tried to remember how Topher's father, Gustav, had behaved at the wedding and reception. He'd been reserved, but that wasn't out of the ordinary for him.

"Why do you bring it up?" Topher asked.

"I don't want to get in the way of your being happy."

Topher snorted. "You're worried that I'll never be happy if I don't have a bunch of puppies to boss around? Do I *seem* like an unhappy dog to you?"

Lashonda's whiskers spread as her mouth curled in a smile. Topher had seemed like a puppy himself all week long. He was the picture of happiness. "No. I just didn't realize. I mean, you never talked about wanting puppies, and I was afraid that my own plans were—I don't know—getting in the way and squashing your dreams."

"My dream is to have that talent scout call me and offer me my own show, back-to-back with The Nightly Howl."

"Yeah, that would be nice," Lashonda said.

Topher must have heard that there was still reservation in her voice because he added, "Look, what did you want to be when you were a kitten?"

"A ballerina," Lashonda said. "And an otter."

Topher barked a laugh. "See? Dreams change."

"Oh, I don't know. I may not be interested in dancing any more, but I still want to be an otter," Lashonda said.

"You're in the wrong field of science then. You should have gone into gene therapy."

The two of them reached the stairs up from the beach and took their concrete steps up to the road. They walked to the bed and breakfast where they were staying and let themselves in with their borrowed keys.

"By the way," Topher whispered in the quiet bed and breakfast, "how is the work on your thesis going?"

Lashonda told Topher about the editing she'd been doing in hushed tones as they walked through the dark halls to their private rooms. But she found herself thinking about how the machine she was designing could be used to print out plastic toys for puppies. When the puppies were done playing, the toys could be melted down again—no mess of toys on the floor and new toys every day, as often as she felt like designing them.

Why wouldn't the images of happy puppies get out of her head?

CHAPTER 3

Married life wasn't a whole lot different than unmarried life for Topher and Lashonda. They'd moved in together several months before the wedding, and, after the honeymoon, they both went back to work. So, their daily routines were largely unchanged.

Even so, Topher would sometimes get a goofy expression in his eyes when he looked at her; and, some days, Lashonda found herself, sitting in the lab at work, twisting her wedding ring around the base of her paw pad, daydreaming away instead of focusing on her experiments.

Mostly Lashonda daydreamed about the hours she'd spent with Topher on their honeymoon, picturing scenes from that idyllic week and savoring them in her memory. Sometimes, she thought with a sense of satisfied pride about the little things they had planned together for the coming evening or weekend —a new recipe for chicken they meant to try, a park where they planned to go for a walk, or a visit to one of their friends.

Some days she thought farther ahead, but that meant worrying about whether the talent scout would finally call Topher or if she'd pass her thesis defense. On her optimistic days when the weather was so beautiful that the sun dazzled her into dreaming crazy dreams, she imagined Topher taking over as the host of The Nightly Howl and herself running her own research lab. Then the phantom puppies came.

Somehow, every time she pictured that perfect future where she and Topher succeeded in their careers beyond their wildest imaginings, they always came home from their jobs to a houseful of puppies.

She pictured tucking the wriggly boys and girls into bed and kissing them each on their fuzzy foreheads, caressing their flopped-over ears, and then saying 'goodnight' before spending a quiet evening with Topher.

It made Lashonda feel mad that she couldn't shake the glowing image of herself mothering a litter of puppies out of her head. She and Topher had agreed before they married that they didn't want the hassle of raising a litter, and he'd told her that his mother's vision of him was out-of-date: he'd moved on. Why couldn't she? Why did her brain keep getting stuck on the image of wiggly tails and wet noses cradled in her arms?

Maybe it was the absurdity of the idea of a mamma cat with puppies that hooked her and kept her thoughts coming back. She knew that she and Topher weren't the first mixed-species couple, but she never saw mixed-species families—no mamma cats with puppies or papa dogs with kittens.

Maybe they stayed home to avoid attention or maybe they were out there—at parks, going on walks—but Lashonda hadn't noticed them because she'd never looked before.

Lashonda decided that if she satisfied her curiosity, the images would, more than likely, go away. So, she started researching adoption, looking up information on the interwebs while waiting for her experiments to run in the lab. She set up the machinery and while she waited for the lasers to charge or the powdered plastics to melt, she searched the interweb.

Lashonda found blogs by adoptive dog parents exploring the travails of raising puppies of a different breed—Bernese

Mountain dogs raising Chihuahua pups; toy poodle puppies raised by Mastiff mothers; Labradors raising Shelties; and Italian Greyhounds raising standard Greyhounds. The pictures of the Greyhound family made Lashonda snicker. All the dogs in that family were shaped the same—long and narrow, gangly legs, and pointed snouts—but the young pups towered over their adoptive parents.

The family portrait of the lesbian Mastiffs with their litter of teacup poodles looked pretty funny too. The pair of giant, butch mothers were so much alike, they could have been twins; the five puppies had their curly white fur done up in pom-pom hair cuts with pink bows tied at the girl's ears and blue bows for the boys. That wouldn't last. As soon as the boys were old enough to talk, they'd refuse to wear ribbons on their ears of any color. Worst of all, the girls were actually wearing *poodle skirts* like ancient humans wore. Lashonda didn't know what their mothers were thinking dressing them that way.

Though, they did keep the most informative blog, so they couldn't be complete fools.

Lashonda knew she shouldn't snicker. She'd look equally ridiculous shepherding around a litter of puppies, no matter the breed. She was getting used to people laughing at her and Topher though. He lived for laughter. He twisted it into his own thing, taking ownership of it. She could do that too. Let them laugh. She would be a mamma cat to a litter of puppies if she wanted to.

With a burst of courage, Lashonda decided that when the rest of the lab techs went away to lunch, she'd actually call the local adoption agency and ask a few questions. That's what the Mastiffs on *Mastiff Mammas, Poodle Pups!* recommended doing if you were serious. Lashonda was hardly serious—she and Topher had barely been married a month, and she was still a graduate student—but she did want more information.

The second half of the morning dragged by as the lab

geared up for a massive test of the synthesizer machine, commonly called the Synth-M. It was shaped a little like a giant copy machine with cannons wired into two of its sides. Those were the lasers. The part shaped like a copy machine opened on the top, and that's where the white powdered plastic could be poured in.

Professor Colten, the tall Irish Setter with curly ears who ran the lab, looked over the work of each technician and grad student, double- and triple-checking to be sure every component was in order. For once, instead of testing the components separately in dry-runs to conserve materials, the whole machine was going to be fired up and used to print out a 3D model of the university. The test would take hours, and, if it worked, the model would be housed in a glass display in the foyer of the college's administration building.

Everyone cheered when the lasers hummed to life. Professor Colten invited them all to join her at a cafe across the street for a celebratory lunch.

After everyone else filed out, Jandrew, the only other feline grad student asked Lashonda, "Aren't you coming?" Jandrew was a tabby who had come to Lashonda and Topher's wedding.

"I'll catch up with you. Order me the halibut sandwich?"

"Sure thing," Jandrew said. He closed the door to the lab behind him.

Once the sound of happy chatting between the other grad students and lab techs drained from the hall, the only sound left was the hum of the lasers as they melted layer after wafer-thin layer of powder inside the Synth-M.

Lashonda dialed up the closest adoption agency on her computer. They answered with audio-only: "Hello, this is Lori at Middlemont Foster and Adoption Center," said a canine voice. "How can I help you?"

"Hi, Lori," Lashonda said, feeling glad the video wasn't on. She was sure the insides of her ears had flushed bright red.

"I've been reading up about puppy adoption and mixed-breed families, and one of the blogs I follow suggested that the best way to get information was to call an actual adoption agency. You guys are the closest, so I called you." After a pause, she added, "My name's Lashonda."

"Well, Lashonda, most of us are out at lunch right now, and I'm only an intern."

Lashonda gritted her teeth. She should have expected that.

"I can try to answer your questions, or, if you like, I could just set up an appointment for your employer to come in and talk to us."

Baffled, Lashonda asked, "My employer?"

"Well, we only set up appointments for prospective parents themselves, but if you want to call back later, you can try talking to someone else over the phone."

"I'm the prospective parent." Lashonda felt extremely strange saying those words. *Prospective parent* wasn't how she saw herself at all. "I have no idea what my employer would have to do with this."

"Oh! I'm sorry," Lori sounded embarrassed. "You sounded like a cat to me. I mean, you have a very feline voice. I hope you're not insulted."

"Not at all," Lashonda said. "I am a cat."

"You are a cat." Lori's voice was hard to read. It sounded like she was trying for deadpan, but her tone carried undertones, subtle nuances of confusion and frustration. Lashonda felt similarly. "Excuse me, Lashonda, but I think you've called the wrong adoption agency. We don't handle kittens, only puppies. You should try the Middlemont Cattery."

"I'm not trying to adopt a kitten," Lashonda said. "My husband is a pug dog, and I thought he'd be happiest raising a litter of puppies."

"A mixed-marriage," Lori said, disgust dripping from her canine voice. "I see. We don't handle those."

Lashonda felt like she'd been punched in the gut. "I told you I was researching mixed-breed adoptions."

"Mixed-breed is no problem," Lori said. Her voice was still filled with disgust. "Mixed-species is another matter. A cat would never be a suitable mother to puppies."

Lashonda was ready to spit, raring to defend herself and the rights she'd only recently come to desire, but she heard the click that meant Lori ended the call. All the anger she felt, readying her for a fight, drained out of her and left her slumped on the desk in front of her computer.

She was still there when Jandrew came back from the celebratory lunch with a cold halibut sandwich wrapped up for her. "What happened?" he asked. "You never came, so I got worried and left early." He looked at the computer screen in front of Lashonda's slumped body and read the words aloud with confusion. "Middlemont Foster and Adoption Center?"

Lashonda twisted her ears backwards but stayed slumped against the desk.

"Are you thinking about becoming a foster parent?" Jandrew asked.

"Apparently not," Lashonda said. "They won't even talk to cats there."

"I thought you didn't want a litter."

"I didn't, but it turns out that Topher does. Maybe."

Jandrew pulled over a chair and sat down beside Lashonda. He put the halibut sandwich on the desk. Its sweet, meaty smell enticed Lashonda. Her ears perked back up, and she unwrapped the sandwich. After a few nibbles, she felt a little more like talking. "Topher says he doesn't care, but I get this feeling that he'd be really happy if he was a father. The more I think about it..." Lashonda was reluctant to admit her feelings, and she chewed over the seasoned halibut while stalling.

Jandrew had never once teased her about dating or marrying a dog. He was reserved, reticent, and possibly the safest person she could think of to tell a secret to. Partly because he wouldn't really care about her secrets—not enough to gossip about them.

"I think I do want to be a mother," Lashonda said. "It goes against everything I thought I knew about myself."

Jandrew was quiet long enough for Lashonda to wonder if he'd have anything to say to her at all. She stole a glance at him over her sandwich. He looked like he was thinking, but he could have been thinking about the Synth-M, humming away behind them.

Finally, his gray-striped ears flicked, and he said, "Why not kittens? Puppies are in high demand, but the catteries are always full of unwanted kittens."

"Why do you know about this?" Lashonda asked.

"I have a sister who's a social worker. She's always ranting about how unreasonable it is that dogs will wait years to adopt a single puppy of their preferred breed when there are whole litters of kittens going without families."

Lashonda blinked. Suddenly, she felt guilty for wanting to adopt puppies instead of kittens. She tried flipping the image in her head, imagining Topher tucking a tiny kitten into bed, kissing her on the forehead instead of herself tucking a wiggly puppy into bed. It felt different. She identified with the kitten in the picture inside her head. How amazing would it have been to be a kitten growing up with a pug dog dad like Topher?

Lashonda loved her dad, but Topher would give an entirely different kind of kittenhood to any litter they adopted, full of hugs and cuddles, jokes and fun. Lashonda knew her father loved her, but he showed it with a quiet pride in her. She remembered telling him that she'd been accepted into grad school. His eyes had shone, and his ears stood taller than she'd ever seen them. But if it were Topher...

He'd sweep a kitten up into a bear hug and smother her

with words of love and kisses. Lashonda felt warm and fuzzy imagining it. She wanted to give that life to a kitten.

"Okay," she said. "I'll think about calling the cattery."

Before she could say more, Lashonda heard the rest of the grad students, all dogs, barking to each other in the hallway. They burst into the room, full of life, energy, and excitement about the Synth-M test underway. The feline lab techs followed behind, much more sedately. Professor Colten was the last to enter the room, shepherding her pack of students and workers back to where they belonged.

"I notice you didn't come to lunch," Professor Colten said to Lashonda.

The other students and lab techs settled into their work stations around the room. A couple of them poked ineffectively at the Synth-M, eager to see if the test was working despite the fact that there was no way to know for sure until they opened it up tomorrow.

"I had something to take care of," Lashonda said diffidently. She was proud to work with Professor Colten on such an important project, but she never felt completely safe around her. Professor Colten, though invited, hadn't come to the wedding.

"Something to take care of? Everything's already taken care of until the test is done. There isn't anything left to do." Professor Colten's tone took on a suspicious edge. "Especially for you, since I know you've already finished and polished every part of your thesis except the experiments section and conclusion." Now she sounded downright hostile.

Lashonda didn't understand why Professor Colten begrudged her getting work done early. Lashonda had made a point of working as far ahead as she could to show that she could keep up with all the dogs. Now it seemed like Professor Colten had decided that made her some sort of show-off. Lashonda didn't know how to win with her.

"It was something personal," she said, quietly. Her ears dipped submissively.

"In the lab?" Professor Colten whuffed, but she didn't press the matter further. She just shook her head, flopping her curly red ears, as if to say that Lashonda was too much for her. A lost cause.

Lashonda's ears dipped lower. She couldn't wait until she graduated.

She loved the Synth-M project, but she hoped that after she had her degree she could get a job in a different lab—maybe a lab with more cats. Or, at least, a dog in charge who didn't dislike her so much. Being married to a dog was one thing; working for one entirely another. It made her fur bristle.

CHAPTER 4

Topher and Lashonda were cuddled on the couch, eating a late dinner of leftover takeout when the phone rang. Topher grabbed the closest audio-receiver and answered. "Yes, this is Topher Brooke." He looked at Lashonda, pantomimed something she didn't understand, and gestured at the open takeout boxes. Into the phone, he said, "This is a fine time to talk."

Lashonda felt a little miffed, but she could tell the call was important. Topher's voice changed tone when he scheduled a gig or talked to someone important in the business—it got deeper and more resonant. His voice had that tone now.

Topher got up from the couch where they'd been eating and took the phone into the other room. Curious, Lashonda turned her ears to continue listening. When she heard him say, "I've been waiting—scratch that, *hoping*—for a call from you," she realized who it must be: The Nightly Howl had finally called! She wasn't sure, but she was almost sure, and her heart started racing for Topher.

Lashonda was too nervous to keep eating. She listened intently to Topher's side of the conversation, but all she heard was information she already knew about Topher's previous experience as a comedian and generic sounds of affirmation.

The takeout grew cold waiting for Topher. Lashonda grew impatient. Then she decided a long phone call was more likely to mean good news and grew patient again. She closed the takeout boxes, put the utensils with a clatter into the sink, and replaced the leftovers in the refrigerator.

"Boo!" Topher said, grabbing her shoulders with his paws from behind. Instinctively, Lashonda's fur puffed out, and she hissed. Topher laughed. "It's just me. There's no one else here."

"I know," she said. "I guess I'm highly strung right now. I'm probably worried about the Synth-M test." Though, she was more worried about Topher's phone call and the fact that she hadn't told him yet about calling the adoption agency. Or the idea of calling a cattery.

"I can understand that. I'm sure it'll be fine." Topher launched into his standard reassurances about how Lashonda was a brilliant scientist and would have no problem getting her PhD until Lashonda's ears began to wander and she couldn't take it anymore.

"Who called?" she asked, interrupting. "Was it The Nightly Howl? It sounded like The Nightly Howl."

Topher's jowls melted into a grin, and the cold pit of nerves in Lashonda's belly melted too. He wouldn't grin like that if it wasn't good news.

"They're giving you your own show!" she guessed, knowing it was a ridiculous guess.

"Uh... no," he said with a look of bemusement and mild confusion. "But they want me to come in and try me for a new segment on The Nightly Howl."

A purr broke into Lashonda's throat, and Topher couldn't help laughing again.

"They like my cat jokes," he said. The look of confusion on

his face deepened. Lashonda knew he had mixed feelings about telling cat jokes. They always got the biggest laughs from dog crowds, and she could hear the irony in them—but he worried he was contributing to the prejudicial atmosphere of their times.

"If they want cat jokes, give them cat jokes. You know I don't mind." Every one of their cat friends who'd seen Topher's act had found his cat jokes hilarious. He delivered them with the perfect edginess to make it sound like he was making fun of the dogs who laughed at his jokes more than the cats themselves. "Besides," Lashonda said, "this is a once in a lifetime opportunity."

Lashonda knew her words would increase the pressure, but Topher did well under pressure. He was a tough dog, and she could see him react positively to the challenge. His jaw set and shoulders squared.

"All right," he said. He jutted his chin out, and his eyes sparkled. The changes were subtle, but Lashonda recognized that he was taking on his stage persona. He was no longer Topher Brooke, her husband; he was Topher Brooke, stand-up comedian and night club performer. He became a whole different person—a character he'd made up—for when he was on stage.

When Topher spoke, his voice came out confident with just the right touch of cheesy exaggeration. "Did you ever wonder what the deal is with hairballs?"

Lashonda smiled; she liked it when he tried out new jokes on her. She felt privileged to be the first one to hear his cleverness.

"I'm telling you," he said, "I've scratched my head about that one. I've wondered and wondered, but I think I've figured it out. It's how cats reproduce!"

Lashonda splayed her ears in puzzlement, but Topher pressed on. He was only partly telling the joke to her; partly, he was telling it to an imaginary room full of dogs who were all hanging on his every word, just out of sight behind the bright light of his imaginary spotlight.

"I mean, what's the difference between a kitten and a hairball, anyway?" he continued. Lashonda could tell he was coming in for the punch line. "They're both useless little balls of fuzz, and our society has way too many of them!" Topher spread his paws dramatically as if presenting his punch line on a silver platter.

Lashonda forced herself to laugh, but her throat caught on the laughter. "See?" she said. "You'll do great. When do they want you to come in?"

As Topher talked about the logistics of his audition, Lashonda told herself over and over again that he didn't really feel that way about kittens. Even so, she decided to put off calling the cattery.

LASHONDA ARRIVED at the lab early the next day after a night filled with dreams about trying to hide soggy, icky, kittens from a strangely monstrous Topher intent on stuffing them down the garbage disposal. She did not feel well rested.

Shouted barks greeted her. The lab techs gathered around the Synth-M, hackles raised, and, on the cats, tails fluffed out like brushes.

"What's going on?" Lashonda asked, feeling her own fur fluff under her lab coat.

"Saboteur!" Archie, the Dachshund lab tech barked.

"The test didn't work," Jandrew said.

Dog eyes stared at Lashonda, and all the cats, except Jandrew, looked diffidently away. None of the other cats would meet her eyes.

"It didn't work?" Lashonda said, measuring the syllables out slowly. "*How* did it not work?" She stepped toward the Synth-

M, lifting onto her tiptoes to see inside the open top. Most of the lab techs and other grad students stepped back, clearing space for her.

Archie growled and held his ground. "Haven't you done *enough* damage?"

Lashonda's ear skewed, but she pushed past Archie, refusing to let his bullying demeanor faze her. She looked into the Synth-M.

Drifts of white plastic powder, the basic building block the machine used, had been pushed to the sides. Most of the powder had clearly already been removed, or it would have filled the Synth-M's interior, completely hiding the scale plastic model of the college they'd hoped to fuse together with criss-crossing lasers on the inside.

Instead, it decorated the model like miniature snow drifts. At least, half of the model. The tiny plastic buildings, complete with all the right colors, stopped halfway high, as if tiny construction crews had tired of building them after laying bricks and hammering 2-by-4s to waist height.

"Did someone turn it off early?" Lashonda asked. She looked at the others, expecting an answer until she realized they weren't looking at her because she'd spoken—they were looking at her because they thought *she* was the answer.

"You're the only one who didn't come to lunch yesterday," Archie growled.

"Yeah, why was that?" a Labrador grad student threw in.

"*Personal reasons*," a calico lab tech hissed. "I heard her say so to Professor Colten."

No one said, "*suspicious*," but Lashonda's ears burned from hearing them all think it.

"Let's check the computer logs," Jandrew said. "Maybe we can calculate when exactly the machine shut down."

Unfortunately for Lashonda, the machine had shut down only an hour after they'd ceremoniously started it the day before, while everyone except for her was away at lunch. Jandrew stood up for her by accusing Archie of faking the computer logs and being the real saboteur. His arguments only threw gasoline on the fire. Lashonda's ears sank lower and lower against her skull as she listened to her colleagues yap and hiss and bark over whether and why she would betray them and the whole Synth-M project. Even with her ears clamped shut, she couldn't help listening to them while she continued to work at the computer, trying to figure out what had gone wrong.

"The lasers overheated," she said. She spoke quietly enough that no one could hear her words, but since they were all arguing about her, they did hear her speak.

"What did you say?" Jandrew asked.

She didn't deign to repeat herself. Instead, she pointed at the computer screen. Jandrew looked over her shoulder and repeated her insight for them all: "The lasers overheated... Oh, that makes sense. We need a stronger cooling mechanism."

All the yapping and hissing gave way to excited discussion of different cooling strategies. The immediate threat to Lashonda's reputation had passed, but the damage to her sense of security was done. She'd seen how quickly her colleagues turned against her.

DURING THE FINAL months of Lashonda's graduate studies, she watched Topher grow more and more excited about his career, as she grew less and less excited about her own.

The rest of her lab focused on brainstorming alternative cooling strategies while Lashonda became increasingly convinced that the answer lay in optimizing the efficiency of all the components of the Synth-M. The design was right, but the execution was sloppy. Greater precision would make the whole machine work better, and it might even allow the machine to be miniaturized for household use instead of the large, institutional machine that took up their entire lab floor.

Of course, the Synth-M wouldn't be Lashonda's project any more once she graduated. Universities almost never hired their own graduate students, preferring to trade for new blood. Lashonda applied for positions at all the industry labs in the area and even a few university labs in other parts of the country, but she felt like she was only going through the motions.

Her interviews with each canine lab supervisor left her cold. During one interview with a Weimaraner in charge of a lab studying nano-fiber cables like those used in the otter space elevator, Lashonda found herself daydreaming about kittens. She wondered if she could build her own miniaturized Synth-M while watching a litter of kittens. How hard could it be to do research and raise kittens at the same time?

When she caught herself, Lashonda tried to refocus on the interview at paw, but she feared the Weimaraner could sense her lack of enthusiasm if not her actual inattention. He would expect passion and excitement from her—any dog would—but she couldn't bring herself to play that game. If extreme competence and proficiency in her field wasn't enough, then maybe she wasn't enough either. Maybe she didn't want to work in a lab anymore.

Despite impeccable marks on her thesis and dissertation defense, very few job offers rolled in.

Meanwhile, Topher's screen tests for The Nightly Howl went well enough that Jeckie Danson, the show's host, decided to give him a one-time shot at doing his shtick live. They flew Topher and Lashonda out to Old York, and Lashonda watched from the live studio audience as shaggy-furred Jeckie Danson, an Old English Sheepdog, introduced Topher Brooke to the television viewers of the entire country.

It gave her the shivers and fluffed her fur to watch Topher

tell his jokes to the entire world—jokes he'd made up and told her, alone in their apartment, in the middle of the night. His jokes felt like secret gifts for her, and it made her proud for so many others to admire them.

Sitting in the studio bleachers, under the harsh lights, surrounded by uproarious laughter, Lashonda realized that none of her job applications would matter anyway. She needed to start over, applying for jobs exclusively in Old York, because that's where she would be living. Topher was going to be a regular on The Nightly Howl. She was sure of it.

The next day, the reviews were unanimous: Topher Brooke was a smash hit among both canine and feline viewers. Cats loved his subtle irony, playacting at making fun of cats while actually making fun of the dumb dogs who make fun of cats. Dogs loved his cat jokes.

Topher and Lashonda moved to Old York

CHAPTER 5

Old York was a city from before time. Skyscrapers built by human hands long before dogs and cats had been uplifted still stood in Old York. The skyscrapers had survived the dark stretch of time after the humans left, before dogs and cats took over the world properly. On the West Coast where both Lashonda and Topher had grown up, human buildings had largely fallen into disrepair and either been knocked down for smaller, more appropriately sized buildings in their place or become abandoned ghost towns.

In Old York, however, dogs and cats lived in the skyscrapers humans had left behind, in rooms with strangely high ceilings, large doors, and uncomfortably spaced steps in the staircases. All the extra space made Lashonda's whiskers twitch, but it would give her room to work on her own version of the Synth-M. And she liked the sense of sitting high above the world that she got from the thirteenth-story and higher windows in the apartments they toured while looking for one of their own. She felt very much like the smug cat sitting in the catbird seat.

While they searched for an available, affordable, aesthetically acceptable apartment, Topher and Lashonda camped out in a rent-by-the-week motel near the docks. Their room had two double beds, a mini-fridge, and not much else. So, they spread out all of the rental applications they picked up on the second bed, like it was some sort of cushy, squishy, annoying desk. White papers, scattered over a worn-out comforter with a strangely dreary floral pattern.

During the days, they ran from one apartment showing to the next, grabbing quick meals in between at corner hot dog carts. Topher never missed a chance to make bad jokes about the unseasonable heatwave in the city meaning he was a hot dog, eating a hotdog. He knew they were bad, but he was off the clock, and even bad jokes generally garnered a few titters from the tourists and made Lashonda smile.

One apartment would be cheap but dismally dark, with only tiny half-windows, way up on the walls, because it was under street level. Another apartment would have beautiful, wide windows with a view of the whole city, but cost far too much. And then there were the weird, quirky apartments that had no walls around the bathroom fixtures or were twenty stories high... without a working elevator. The best apartments were completely crowded with prospective renters during their showings, and invariably, they seemed to go to one of the pure-bred dog couples who applied, not Topher and Lashonda.

By the end of their first week in the motel, Topher had to start his job at the Nightly Howl, and they hadn't found a place yet. So, Lashonda found herself bouncing around the city alone, checking out apartments and forcing herself to imagine what Topher would think of them, as well as figuring out what she thought. He cared more about convenience and location, less about windows and floor space.

Then at night, she sat in the motel room, watching the Nightly Howl, snacking on bags of tuna chips, and filling out applications. Alone. She wouldn't be able to get to work on her own version of the Synth-M until they were settled, so she had a strong incentive to give up and pick an apartment, even if it was a little wonky.

By the end of the second week, Lashonda lucked into a finding an apartment that was nearly perfect, except the cat who'd lived there for the last decade had been heavily into pickled herring, and the smell had soaked into the floorboards and walls. No dog wanted it, and few cats could afford it. But Topher was used to Lashonda's fishy snack foods, and she knew he wouldn't mind. She snapped the place up before he'd even had a chance to see it.

Life got a lot better when they had an address that Lashonda's sister could ship their boxes to, and they were finally able to unpack, settle in, and start turning a tiny corner of the big city into a home.

Topher was making enough money from his job with the Nightly Howl and the apartment was cheap enough that Lashonda decided to postpone looking for a job herself. She had too many ideas she wanted to explore about how to improve the Synth-M, and none of the labs she'd talked to were willing to let her work on her own project. She could always look for a job again after building her own synthesizer. In fact, she'd probably be in a better position to negotiate.

Lashonda fell into a daily routine. She woke up early and worked on the designs for her household-sized synthesizer on her computer while watching the sun rise between the buildings through her apartment's glorious windows. As the morning waned, she fell into cruising the interweb for cattery websites, and lost herself looking at the pictures and bios of all the adoptable kittens.

The majority of the kittens were tabbies, torbies, and calicos, striped and splotched. Occasionally she found a few kittens who looked like young Lashondas—their eyes looked like green or gold gems staring out from a face of blackest midnight. The kittens who appealed to Lashonda most, though, were the very rare Siamese, Burmese, and Himalayan kittens. Their bios invariably said that they were already undergoing the process of being adopted—probably because they were purebred or, at least, looked that way. What Lashonda liked about them was that their markings—light fur that darkened on their ears, muzzles, and paws—made her think of Topher's coloring. Perhaps it was shallow, only fur-deep, but she liked that they looked a little like both her and him.

When Topher woke, around lunchtime, Lashonda hurriedly closed all the incriminating websites on her computer. She couldn't bring herself to admit to Topher that her view on having a litter had changed so drastically, so quickly. She had trouble even admitting it to herself.

Lashonda and Topher ate lunch together, but then he left for the offices of The Nightly Howl. Even though his bit of the show only lasted two to three minutes per episode, he spent all day working with the writers, brainstorming new jokes, and rehearsing before the studio audience. At ten o'clock every night, they filmed live. He came home late, but Lashonda tried to stay up for him. It was difficult, since she couldn't break her habit of waking early.

During the afternoons, Lashonda explored the streets of Old York. It was a giant city. Giant buildings built by giants. She walked aimlessly amongst the tall buildings that had been designed for the larger scale of the humans who had built them, all the while mapping out the circuitry in her head for her household-sized synthesizer. It was growing ever closer to reality. She returned home with armfuls of groceries—some for dinner, others with materials for building the synthesizer.

Wires, circuit boards, metal casings, screwdrivers, and a

soldering iron littered the floor of their apartment. Lashonda constructed her prototype machine, piece by piece, as the windows grew dark, and the television blared nighttime shows in the background. She left the television running for the noise and company, but when The Nightly Howl started, she put her tools aside. She watched Topher through the tiny screen as if he were looking right at her, as if his goofy grin between jokes was meant for her alone.

The cat jokes didn't bother Lashonda; she hadn't lied when she told Topher that. However, one night the topic du jour on the Nightly Howl was catteries. A moderately famous, or perhaps infamous, young Chihuahua, heiress to the owner of Moonville Funpark, had made a big splash in the news trying to adopt a kitten. Jeckie Danson made fun of her mercilessly throughout the hour-long show. As always, Topher's bit was themed to the rest of the show, and Lashonda watched in horror as he told his kittens and hairballs joke, fleshed out into an entire three minute routine bashing kittens and catteries.

For the first time, Lashonda lost her firm hold on the belief that Topher's jokes were satire, nothing more. Her walls tumbled down, and she felt like every dog in the world was laughing at her. Lashonda mixed herself a Long Island Catnip Tea and fell asleep in front of her computer, cruising cattery websites.

"What's this?" Topher asked, laying a gentle paw on Lashonda's shoulder.

She awoke blearily and refocused her eyes on the computer screen in front of her. A pair of angelic blue eyes stared back at her. It was the picture of an adoptable tabby from a litter of five; three girls, two boys; all sporting non-descript gray tabby stripes and, according to their bios, "bright, cheerful, immediately loveable" dispositions.

"I... uh..." Lashonda started, but the computer screen in front of her said it all.

"You're looking at cattery websites? Is this about the routine I did tonight? You know I was just joking."

Relief flooded Lashonda. She had known, really, but it helped to hear him say it. "No," she said. "I've been looking at cattery websites for months."

"I thought you didn't want a litter," Topher said.

"I didn't," she said.

Topher waited. Apparently, he wasn't going to make this easy for her. She wished he would see into her heart, realize how she felt, and say that he understood. Then she wouldn't have to explain. But, while Topher was clever, he was better at joking about cats than understanding them. He loved her; that didn't mean he understood her.

"I changed my mind," she said. She thought about explaining the months that she'd spent staring at pictures of kittens, imagining their lives and futures with each one of them. She considered telling him that she didn't want to deny a dog who'd be such a good father the chance to be one. She could have told him how much it would mean for a cattery kitten to have a family at all, let alone a dog like Topher for a father. There were too many things she could say that were all part of the truth. None of them were all of it. In the end, part of what Lashonda loved about Topher is that he didn't make her explain. He accepted her simple answer at face value: she had changed her mind.

"Okay..." he said. His brow furrowed into wrinkled folds. "You want to adopt a kitten?"

Lashonda's voice grew small, her ears tipped back, and she asked, "Are you okay with that?"

Topher looked at the picture of the kitten on the screen. His brown canine eyes locked on the feline blue ones. "Are you sure you aren't just lonely?"

"Yes," she said. For the first time, Lashonda wondered whether Topher really had changed his mind about wanting to be a father. Or was it just that he didn't want to be a father to kittens?

"Now?" he asked. The word ended in a strangled sound.

Lashonda knew they'd been married barely a year. It was early to think about children, even if they were a normal couple who'd planned on having a litter all along. Still, she couldn't help feeling that the time was right. Topher's job was solid; staying home with kittens wouldn't interrupt her career as she was working independently anyway.

"It would take time," she said, "to go through the adoption process."

Topher laughed. "So, yes, now." He shook his head. "And people think I'm the funny one. Look, Lash, I need to think about it. This is about as thorough of a one-eighty degree turn as you could pull on me. I don't change gears that fast."

Lashonda dipped her ears and nodded, meaning full well to be patient with Topher and give him the time he needed. However, once the flood gates opened, she could talk to him about nothing else. They stayed up until dawn, talking about kittens.

Every day at lunch and then again when Topher came home from The Nightly Howl, Lashonda filled his ears with her thoughts on kittens—what size litter would be best; whether a mix of boys and girls was better or a single-gender litter like her and her sisters; if it was better to adopt newborns or kittens who'd been in the cattery awhile. Topher had fewer thoughts, but the opinions he offered didn't contradict her vision of a future filled with kittens.

By the end of the week, Topher agreed that they should make an appointment with the closest cattery. He had put aside the dream of being a father when he'd met Lashonda, but, in the face of her enthusiasm, the old dream came back again, albeit in a slightly new shape. Whatever reservations he may or may not have felt about fathering kittens instead of puppies, he kept to himself.

~

THE SEARCHING HEART Cattery was housed on the fifteenth floor of a tall gray building with a Thai restaurant at ground level, sandwiched between a sketchy looking health clinic on the fourteenth floor and a martial arts studio above. The walls inside the front office were decorated with crayon drawings and framed portraits of kittens with big, soulful eyes. The tile floor was decorated with paw prints done in bright, primary colors. Lashonda rang the bell at the empty front desk.

A harried looking tortoiseshell-furred woman wearing coveralls with cotton print patch pockets came in through the door behind the desk. "Are you Lashonda Brooke?" she asked. "I'm Roseanne. Come on in."

Lashonda and Topher followed Roseanne through the door, and she launched right into a whirlwind tour of the cattery. She led them past a crowded room of cots strewn with drab blankets and ratty toys that had clearly seen years and years of use. They looked in at the windowed door of a room that the Roseanne called the "school room." Toddler kittens played inside under the watchful eyes of several troublingly young adult tabbies and one elderly calico. Lashonda thought the adults, except for the calico, looked younger than her.

"The older kittens, of course," Roseanne said, "go to the public school in this district. It's five blocks that way." She pointed out the nearest window; it faced the windows of another twenty story building. "All right, then, let's sit down and chat." She led them back to the front office and gestured for them to sit in a pair of chairs facing the front desk.

"Are we going to meet any of the kittens?" Topher asked.

"No. Not on your first visit." She sat down behind the desk, suddenly brusque and businesslike.

"There's a process," Lashonda said.

"That's right. We don't like to get the kittens' hopes up." Roseanne eyed Topher meaningfully as he sat down. "We don't get a lot of dogs here." Her eyes narrowed, and her ears flicked, almost too briefly to notice. "Why don't you tell me a bit about the path that brought you here?"

Lashonda wasn't sure where to start, but, to her surprise, she didn't have to. Topher took the lead.

"I always wanted to be a father, but then I met a mysterious black cat who bewitched me into believing she didn't ever want to be a mother." He looked over at Lashonda and took one of her paws in his own. "I fell madly in love with her and gave up my foolish dreams of fatherhood. Then, suddenly, after we'd been married for about a year, she told me that she wanted to adopt a litter of kittens."

Lashonda swished her tail and dipped her ears. "You make me sound completely whimsical, like I change my mind at the drop of a hat."

"Lashy, dear, there is a reason I do not wear hats. You're confusing enough as it is; I can't imagine what would happen to me if I had a hat falling off my head all the time, and with my lumpy head, you know it would fall off." Topher shook his head, flapping his ears and jowls comically.

Roseanne snorted then looked flustered trying to regain her dignity after her unintended laughter.

"I'd been thinking about adoption for months," Lashonda said. "He just didn't notice." She glared at Topher, daring him to disagree with her, but he knew better than that.

Lashonda told Roseanne about her experience with the Middlemont Foster and Adoption Center, the work she was doing from home on a synthesizer, and how she'd come to have trouble imagining her future without a litter of kittens in it.

Occasionally, Topher threw in a joke, but when it came to serious thoughts he'd already said his part.

As Roseanne and Lashonda were wrapping up and discussing the next step in the process, the elderly calico from the school room poked her head in the door.

Roseanne saw her and said, "Hey guys, this is Ayla. She's top cat around here. And, Ayla, this is Lashonda and Topher."

Ayla smiled with her whiskers, but the smile didn't reach her eyes. Her eyes stared piercingly at Topher. "You're familiar," she said.

Roseanne whispered, "The Nightly Howl."

Ayla's eyes narrowed further.

"I didn't realize you'd recognized me," Topher said. He looked flattered. Lashonda, however, had a sinking feeling that everything was about to go wrong.

"You're that dog who makes fun of cats," Ayla said. It wasn't a question, more of an accusation. Ayla turned to Roseanne and said, "Can I speak with you for a minute?" The two of them stepped out of the front office, and Lashonda could hear the sharp tone of Ayla's voice through the closed door. When Roseanne came back, she looked sad.

"I'm sorry," she said. "I don't think you're going to find any kittens who are a good match for you here."

Lashonda's ears folded back. She felt the same mix of anger, shame, and confusion in the pit of her stomach that she'd felt when the dog at the Middlemont Foster and Adoption Center had told her a cat could never be a proper mother for puppies.

"What happened?" Topher asked. "I thought everything was going well."

Roseanne's ears dipped down. She didn't want to tell them, but she didn't have to. Lashonda understood all too well what had happened, and she translated for Topher. "They think that because you make fun of cats on television that you shouldn't be allowed to adopt kittens." Lashonda felt horrible telling him that, and she could see in his eyes that it hit him hard deep down.

"For what it's worth," Roseanne offered, "I think you're hilarious. Satire is lost on Ayla. Well, most humor is lost on Ayla."

Roseanne recommended several other catteries they could try in the surrounding area and sent them on their way.

CHAPTER 6

The days and weeks added up as Lashonda and Topher made appointments with the other catteries and waited for them to happen. The weeks and months added up as those appointments came and went, each telling the same story.

The social workers at some catteries were more direct and honest than others. Like Roseanne they simply turned Lashonda and Topher away. Others strung them along, letting them work through the cattery's adoption processes until she and Topher would suddenly meet a dead end: *not approved*.

Lashonda kept in touch with Roseanne. She'd call and ask for her advice about which cattery to try next and how to handle the social workers at any given cattery. Roseanne knew most of them. Eventually, during a call to discuss the catteries on the Lower Eastside, Lashonda broke down and confided in Roseanne that she didn't think a cattery would ever let Topher adopt a kitten.

"And I'll never be allowed to adopt a puppy. Even if Topher quit the Nightly Howl," Lashonda said, "he'd still be the dog who *used to* tell jokes about cats. I never thought I'd regret his choice of career."

Roseanne grew quiet on the other end of the line.

"Look, I'm sorry," Lashonda said. "You've been really helpful, but I think it's time to give up." Lashonda looked at her partially de-constructed synthesizer, filling the living room floor of her apartment. It was surrounded by plastic test objects that had synthesized fine and then drooped like melting candles afterward. A fine sprinkling of white plastic synthesis powder covered the carpet.

The synthesizer was so close to working. If she could find a lab that would take her and her project on, then she'd have access to more powerful computers and could figure out what was going wrong. She could refocus her life on her work. That was what she should do.

That idea had never seemed hollow before.

She would have to tell Topher. The worst part was, she knew he would take it well. He'd try to comfort her, even though he'd be hurting inside.

Roseanne spoke again, her voice reluctant, "There's a name I'm going to give you: Dr. Jacqueline Flockhart. She's a dog who called here looking for mixed-species couples who want to have a litter. She's been calling all the catteries in the area. I haven't mentioned her before, because, honestly, she sounds a little crazy. But... as a last resort... Well, you might want to try giving her a call."

Lashonda took down Dr. Flockhart's contact information and thanked Roseanne. She wondered why a doctor would be seeking out couples looking to adopt. Perhaps she handled cases of litters with extreme special health needs. Lashonda wasn't sure if she and Topher were prepared to sign on for something like that. Still, it couldn't hurt to call.

The area code for Dr. Flockhart's number was unusual, so Lashonda looked it up. Apparently, her offices were located on an artificial island, a seastead off the coast of Old York, created to avoid the laws of the mainland. As far as Lashonda could tell, no one lived or worked on Friedan Isle if they weren't doing something illegal. She wasn't sure she liked the sound of that.

Curiosity piqued, Lashonda called the number using full video, but the secretary who answered used only the audio channel.

"Hello," the voice said. "You've reached the offices of Dr. Jacqueline Flockhart. This is Kevin speaking."

Lashonda couldn't tell from his voice whether Kevin was a cat or a dog. Normally, that wouldn't bother her, but she knew so little about Dr. Flockhart and was seeking answers to questions so large that she found it quite disconcerting.

"Er, hi, my name is Lashonda, and a social worker—Roseanne with the Searching Heart Cattery—gave me this number. She said, maybe you could help me."

"Maybe," Kevin said. "Can you tell me a little more?"

"Sure..." Lashonda wasn't sure exactly what Kevin was looking for, so she simply started to explain her situation. "See, I'm a cat, and my husband is a dog. We'd like to adopt a litter, but no one will work with us. Dogs don't trust a cat to be a mother to puppies, and the catteries..." Lashonda trailed off, suddenly tired. She didn't know why she was telling her troubles to this secretary. She didn't even know what he could do for her. "I'm sorry. My friend suggested I call you, but I don't even know what Dr. Flockhart does. Can you please tell me?"

Kevin cleared his throat before speaking. "Dr. Flockhart leads a team of independent researchers on Frieden Isle investigating gene therapy and in vitro fertilization for revolutionary outcomes." The words sounded canned, as if Kevin had practiced saying them many times.

"Revolutionary outcomes? What does that mean?"

"It means that if Dr. Flockhart's research succeeds, it could change the world."

Lashonda's fur bristled. "I know what the word 'revolutionary' means, but what sort of research is it?"

"Gene therapy and in vitro fertilization."

Lashonda felt like Kevin was trying to make a fool of her and seriously considered hanging up on him. Instead she asked, "Why would that involve calling Old York catteries looking for mixed-species couples?"

"We are looking for a few serious test subjects," he said, his voice grown careful and measured. "If you'd like to be considered for that, then we could run background checks on you and your husband to see if you're suitable."

Lashonda wondered what kind of research was so crazy that they'd need to do it on an island with an independent government and run background checks before being willing to talk straight about it. She also wondered how crazy she'd have to be to sign on for something like that.

Of course, she could always back out later. "Sure. What do you need from me?"

During the rest of the call, Kevin asked a lot of questions without offering a lot of answers. Lashonda felt like she was being interrogated, and her mind began to drift to images of bizarre biological research as she fed Kevin the rote answers to his questions. *What did gene therapy and in vitro fertilization add up to? Cats with wings? Dogs who never needed to sleep? Probably it was something mundane like a treatment for kittens or puppies with childhood leukemia. Important but depressing work with terminally ill infants.* Finally, Kevin promised to get back to her if she and Topher qualified for the program and ended the call.

Given her experiences with the catteries and Middlemont Foster and Adoption Center, Lashonda didn't expect to hear from Kevin again. She was disappointed that she might never know what Dr. Flockhart's mysterious program involved. Maybe she'd see it in the news some day.

LASHONDA DIDN'T TELL TOPHER about Dr. Flockhart. She didn't tell him that she'd given up on the catteries either. She only told him that she needed a break for a while; the constant rejection was too depressing.

Maybe Topher had been right, and she didn't really want to be a mother; she was simply lonely. A few vid-calls with her sisters per week hardly replaced actually seeing them, and she hadn't made any real friends. She had been painfully isolated since moving to Old York.

Now that Adelle was busy with a new litter of kittens, and Sherri and Kelly were busy helping her, even the vid-calls were starting to die off. Kelly urged Lashonda to come visit, but she didn't feel right visiting where Topher wasn't welcome. And she knew Adelle wouldn't want a rough and tumble dog—even Lashonda's husband—anywhere near her precious babies.

Despondent, Lashonda began querying nearby laboratories. Working with colleagues again would revitalize her, and, maybe, it would take her mind off of the phantom kittens that were slowly fading out of her vision of the future, leaving behind kitten-shaped holes where they had been.

Lashonda interviewed with a dozen different laboratories in the surrounding area, voyaging further and further away by train with each one. She was serious about finding a position, so she showed all the enthusiasm that any dog could ask for. Yet, every interview culminated in the same question: "Why have you been working alone for the last year?"

Lashonda brought folders of documentation showing the work she'd accomplished on her own, but none of the dogs in charge wanted to see that. They weren't interested in the work she'd done. They were interested in knowing if she could be a team player, and her year of isolated research suggested that she might not really have a team mind set.

Lashonda looked for laboratories run by cats, but she couldn't find any. There were laboratories run by otters, but they were all far away in Europe or on the space station. She found one that sounded promising on Friedan Isle, but it wasn't hiring. Lashonda daydreamed about moving to Deep Sky Anchor, the otter space station in geosynchronous orbit above the space elevator, but Topher's job was in Old York, half a hemisphere away and firmly on the Earth's surface.

Lashonda wondered whether there were otter pups on the space station in need of adoption and whether the otters were any less restrictive about mixed-species families than her own culture. She doubted it.

BY THE TIME Dr. Flockhart's office called back, nearly two months had passed. She recognized the number, because of the unusual area code. She was surprised when she answered to be greeted by full video: the image of a small dog, perhaps a terrier, with wiry gray hair stared at her from the vid-screen. He was seated at a desk piled high with papers and manila folders, and when he spoke Lashonda recognized Kevin's voice. "Hello? I'm calling for Lashonda or Topher Brooke."

"I didn't expect to hear from you again."

A thin smile split Kevin's muzzle. "You must be Lashonda."

"Yes." Lashonda's voice was cold, but sparks of excitement already threatened to consume her. She thought she'd moved on. Apparently she hadn't.

"There is an opening in Dr. Flockhart's program, and our research suggests that you and your husband might be suitable. If you're still interested, I can make an appointment for you."

Lashonda's ears burned as she tried to contain her temper. "You want us to come out to Friedan Isle for an appointment without even knowing what exactly Dr. Flockhart does?"

The thin smile on Kevin's muzzle turned to a frown, and there was sympathy in his eyes. "How long have you been looking for a litter to adopt?" Lashonda tallied up the months in her head. *Had it only been a year? It felt longer.* Before she could answer, Kevin continued. "My wife is a cat. She had a litter with her first husband, so I haven't gone through what you've been going through, but a lot of us with Dr. Flockhart are mixed-species couples. I promise you, if you come meet Dr. Flockhart, you'll find her work unlike anything you've encountered so far. She could make a big difference for people like us."

Lashonda narrowed her green eyes. "Okay," she said. "How soon can we have an appointment?"

CHAPTER 7

The tall Old York buildings cast long shadows in the early light of dawn. The ground was slippery with rain and oil under paw, and the morning air was chill enough to nip at Lashonda through her fur and jacket.

"Why do we have to get up this early again?" Topher asked. He held Lashonda's paw but dragged behind her. She hurried on anyway, pulling him toward the entrance to the underground train station. He was not a morning person, and waking him up had already got them off to a late start.

"We have to take a train to the docks," Lashonda said, not pausing to look at him. "And the ferry to Friedan Isle only leaves three times a day. If we don't catch the first ferry, we'll miss our appointment. I told you that last night."

"Yes, but why do we have to go to Friedan Isle?" Topher continued to lumber along, much slower than Lashonda would have liked. "There are plenty of catteries we haven't tried on the mainland. Old York is a big city."

"This isn't a cattery," Lashonda said.

They descended, finally, down the stairs toward the underground trains, and the natural light of dawn gave way to the timeless, artificial light of the surreal network of tunnels beneath the city. Unlike the ferry, the trains ran every fifteen minutes. One was waiting at the station as soon as they arrived, and they were able to board immediately.

Lashonda relaxed a little once they were seated on the red vinyl benches of the train.

"If it's not a cattery," Topher said, "where are we going?"

Lashonda flexed her claws nervously, just to feel them stretch. "It's a doctor. Roseanne gave me the number of this doctor who was looking for mixed-species couples, cats and dogs trying to adopt litters. All I know is she does gene therapy and in vitro fertilization."

Topher appeared to be mulling that over. While he thought, the train car filled up with other cats and dogs on their way to work. Once all the seats filled, passengers continued to file onto the train and were forced to stand in the center, holding the poles. A happy Newfoundland crowded Lashonda, his tail wagging. The Newfoundland apologized, but his brushy tail kept flapping against her with each wag. A brown tabby cat sitting across the way rolled her eyes at the Newfoundland and shared a look with Lashonda.

Why was he so happy? Lashonda wondered. *Wagging his tail like that?* She hated the crowds on the train, but all the dogs looked happy, shoved against each other, jostling one and another every time the train lurched to a start or stop. All the dogs except Topher. He still looked pensive.

Lashonda leaned close to him and said, "What are you thinking?" It felt weird talking in public about their private lives, but she didn't think anyone was listening. Besides, it would be hard to hear a single conversation over the noise of the tracks and the general hubbub of so many bodies pressed together.

"Well, if this doctor is studying in vitro fertilization," Topher said, keeping his voice low and slow like hers, "then does that mean she'd be planning to use you to carry a litter? That she's studying?"

Lashonda's ears twitched. She hadn't thought of that. She'd never planned on being pregnant. That wasn't part of adopting.

Topher continued: "Whose litter would it be? Would it be yours? *Who else's?*" He stopped for a moment, and his voice dropped even lower. "I don't know how I feel about you carrying some tom's litter that I don't know. It's one thing to adopt a litter together, but watching you have some other guy's litter? That doesn't seem right. Unless..."

Lashonda waited as the noise of the train filled Topher's silence. Sometimes, if she waited long enough, he'd finish his thoughts. He thought things through more slowly than she did. She knew that, but it was hard to wait. She took his paw and squeezed it. "Unless what?"

"Well, it's crazy, but why do you think this doctor is looking for mixed-species couples? You don't think..."

Listening to Topher think through the situation with Dr. Flockhart reminded Lashonda of how it felt for her to talk to Kevin on the phone. All questions; no answers. "Think what?" she prompted.

Topher's brown eyes looked intense and wild as he said, "Hybrids. Dog-cat hybrids."

Lashonda blinked, too surprised even for her ears to twitch.

"I said it was crazy." Topher chuckled as if he'd been joking, but Lashonda knew better.

After a while she said, nearly in a whisper, "I like your guess better than mine."

Until he answered, she wasn't even sure if Topher had heard. "What's your guess?"

"Terminally sick children." She felt sick herself as she said it. She still wasn't sure if she could handle that. She didn't know where exactly her limits fell. Was a dying litter better than no litter? What if it was a litter that needed her? More questions, and these ones had hard answers that she'd have to find inside herself. She wasn't sure she wanted to know those answers.

She'd feel cold and heartless if she was unwilling to open her heart to kittens who needed her unless they were healthy. Was it selfish to only want healthy children? On the other paw, she'd feel like a fool, choosing to mire her heart in a sinking swamp of pain for the rest of her life when she could choose to avoid it.

Topher squeezed back on her paw and said, "But you made the appointment anyway, huh?"

Their eyes met, and Lashonda could see what he was thinking. He thought she'd decided already: she'd rather care for terminally ill kittens than no kittens. "It's just for information," she said. "We can always back out."

"Right." He didn't say it like he was agreeing with her, merely acknowledging that she needed to believe what she was saying. For now. He squeezed her paw tight.

Lashonda realized that he would back her decision if she wanted to enter into Dr. Flockhart's program, even if it involved binding their hearts to kittens who were sick or dying. She'd started this whole journey because she wanted to bring happiness into Topher's life, but somehow it had turned into a voyage of sadness. She hoped that his crazy idea—dog-cat hybrids— was closer to the truth than her guess, because she feared that he was right, and she wouldn't back out, not from the only chance they had left.

The rest of their train ride passed in the relative silence of a halted conversation, heavy with implications. They arrived at the docks with twenty minutes before the morning ferry to Friedan Isle and used the time to grab a quick breakfast to go from a dockside diner, bacon-and-egg sandwiches.

They rode on the open deck of the ferry and ate their sandwiches. The ocean breeze felt salty in Lashonda's whiskers and damp on her fur. She watched the giant Statue of the First

Race, a human woman made from green copper and clothed in flowing robes with one arm held high, loom above as they sailed through the glassy, green water of the bay.

The ancient statue was a testament to all the great accomplishments of the humans during their time on the Earth. Many dogs believed that the humans, or the First Race, had great, godlike plans for the animals they'd uplifted. Others believed that humans had been merely another species like dogs and cats themselves. Lashonda wasn't sure what to believe, but she wondered what humans would think of a canine doctor meddling with the genes of the creatures they'd uplifted—whether it was to cure some disease or break down the species barrier between cats and dogs.

The glassy, green water of the bay, edged by skyscrapers, gave way to the choppy, gray water of the open ocean. Wind whipped their whiskers, and Lashonda suggested that they move from the deck to inside the ferry. Yet, she continued to watch the ocean as they sailed. Over the next hour, the distant seastead—at first, merely an amber dimple on the platinum surface of the ocean—grew larger and more distinct.

At first, it grew facets like a gemstone reflecting the light at many angles, shining and throwing off sparks of sun. Then, the facets resolved into the slanted walls and roofs of skyscrapers, much like the buildings in Old York, only rising from the ocean, isolated on the horizon and topped with tiny windmills that sparkled as their golden blades turned in the whipping wind. Also, these skyscrapers were packed much more tightly together, and sky bridges laced between them, tying all the buildings into one giant honeycomb structure.

When the ferry arrived at Friedan Isle, it sailed right between the buildings and into a small bay, encircled by the golden skyscrapers. Instead of rising out of a solid island beneath them, like Lashonda had expected, the buildings rose straight out of the ocean, and rivulets of ocean water flowed between them. Whatever moored the buildings together and buoyed them up was invisible underneath the lapping, blue water.

Lashonda was also surprised to find that the buildings' amber-gold color wasn't merely a reflection of the late morning sun. It had to do with the material they were made from. Topher asked some of the other dogs on the ferry's deck and was told that the golden material was solar paneling. Between the solar panels and the windmills, Friedan Isle powered itself completely and independently of any other nation.

"This is an amazing place," Lashonda whispered, feeling strangely awed by the golden city and its blue rivers that surrounded her. "Why don't we hear about it more?"

The dog who'd told Topher about the solar panels, a Bloodhound, heard her and said, "It's an otter city, and most of the news channels back home don't like to admit how great otter technology is. It's bad enough that they have the space elevator and Deep Sky Anchor. If people knew about everything the otters have... Well, things would change."

Lashonda blinked at the Bloodhound.

"Not everybody likes change," he added with a shrug.

"What kind of change?" Lashonda asked, but the Bloodhound had stopped paying attention. The ferry had pulled up to a dock beside one of the buildings, and one of the members of the crew was raising a gangway to the pier.

Topher and Lashonda exited with the other passengers, mostly business dogs and the occasional cat dressed in a suit. The cats, except for Lashonda, had all ridden inside the ferry's passenger compartment. One of them, a large orange tom, held paws with a dainty Chihuahua woman wearing a garishly pink, strappy dress under a maroon sweater.

"I wonder if they're going to Dr. Flockhart's, too," Lashonda said.

"We could ask," Topher said.

Lashonda shook her head, feeling too nervous about their appointment to talk to anyone she didn't know, but Topher was looking at the couple and didn't see her. "Hey!" he called to them. "This is a long shot, but we're looking for a Dr. Flockhart's offices. Do you know where it is?"

"We're going there, too!" the Chihuahua woman barked. She looked Topher and Lashonda over. After a moment, she gave them a big grin and said, "Want to walk with us? We'll show you the way."

The orange tom holding her paw looked uncomfortable, but Topher didn't notice that. "Absolutely!" Topher said.

Paved pathways ran along the edges of the buildings, beside the rivulets of ocean water. As the two cats and two dogs walked together down the pathways, Lashonda watched small boats in the water ferry other cats and dogs about. The deeper they worked their way into the floating city, the more small boats there were all leaving wakes behind on the otherwise smooth water. Then, Lashonda noticed a smaller wake, and, at the head of it, a small dome of brown fur. In fact, it was an otter's head.

The otter swam to the side of the rivulet where he climbed a ladder out of the water and onto the paved walkway. He stood on the walkway, dripping in a three-piece suit. Lashonda had to stop herself from laughing. She had never seen an otter in real life before, only on the television.

"Hey, Topher," she said, meaning to point out the otter to him, but he was deep in conversation with the Chihuahua woman.

They walked a little farther, and Lashonda began to see otters everywhere—swimming in the rivulets, walking on the pathways, steering the boats, and dining at the sidewalk cafes at the bases of the tall, golden buildings. Most of the otters dripped, leaving wet trails on the pavement and puddles under their chairs at the sidewalk cafes. Though, the bright sunlight, bouncing between the reflective skyscrapers, soon dried their tracks.

The Bloodhound had said Friedan Isle was an otter city, but Lashonda hadn't realized how literally he meant it.

Eventually the Chihuahua woman guided them into one of the golden-paneled buildings with a plain facade toward the walkway—no colorful parasols to shade inviting cafe tables here. The four of them got into an elevator, and, in the enclosed space, Lashonda started actually listening to the dogs' conversation.

"No hard feelings, then?" Topher said.

"Are you kidding?" the Chihuahua answered. "Jeckie Danson has devoted a whole episode of his show to making fun of me at least once a year since my high school graduation. If I didn't have a sense of humor about it, I'd have given up and moved to the otter space station long ago."

"So, I guess that kitten adoption didn't end up working out for you, eh?"

"Cattery social workers won't take me seriously," she said. "They think I'm still the flighty teenager who was all over the news five years ago."

Lashonda looked closer at the Chihuahua. Her face was fawn colored except for the milk-white markings around her muzzle that stretched into a perfectly symmetrical, spoon-shape on her forehead; her eyebrow fur had been dyed pink to match her dress; and her ears were studded with pink gemstone piercings. Lashonda couldn't believe she hadn't recognized her sooner. She was Vienne Howard, daughter of the billionaire dog who owned Moonville Funpark.

The elevator opened, revealing the same desk Lashonda had seen on the vid-phone when Kevin called to book her appointment, complete with the wiry gray-haired dog sitting behind it.

Vienne and her orange tom husband checked in with

Kevin, and he told them Dr. Flockhart was ready for them. They could go right back.

Suddenly, Vienne turned to Lashonda. "Is this your first appointment?" she asked.

Lashonda nodded.

Vienne reached out and clasped Lashonda's paws, startling her. "Good luck!" she said. "I hope Dr. Flockhart accepts you into the program. If so, we may be seeing a lot more of each other!"

Lashonda wasn't sure how she felt about overtures of friendship from Vienne Howard, but she didn't have time to worry about it. As soon as Vienne and her husband disappeared through one of the doors in the back of the room, Kevin greeted her and Topher. He had paperwork for them to fill out and gestured toward several chairs and a couch over to the side of the room where they could work on it.

Sitting in the waiting area, Lashonda studied the paperwork. It was filled with questions about her and Topher's medical histories. She knew that she was coming to see a doctor, but Lashonda hadn't thought of Dr. Flockhart as a doctor for her, just for the litter she hoped to adopt.

As she scribbled the answers to Dr. Flockhart's invasive questions on page after page of paper, Lashonda felt her excitement rising. Why *would* Dr. Flockhart need all this information and why would she need mixed-species couples, if she *wasn't* breeding cat-dog hybrids? In a golden city where otters swam through the streets and the heiress of Moonville Funpark wanted to make friends with her, anything seemed possible.

SEVERAL HOURS LATER, Lashonda sat uncomfortably on an examining table, white paper beneath her and wrapped around her in the form of a sheet pulled up to her waist and a silly gown that covered her shoulders and chest. The paper gown crinkled against her fur. The stark contrast between its whiteness and the black of her own fur reminded Lashonda absurdly of her wedding dress. Lashonda didn't wear white often for a reason. It was too striking on her. Or dresses, for that matter. She felt much more comfortable in a simple vest and pants. There was nothing good about a white paper gown.

"We should have bought some sandwiches for lunch when we picked up breakfast at that diner," Topher said. He was seated on a bench on the opposite side of the small room, leaned against the wall. The nurses—a black cat like herself and a chatty yellow Labrador—had run tests on him, too, but they were already done. He got to be fully clothed.

Lashonda had spent all morning being quizzed, poked, prodded, and tested by nurses and underlings. She'd had her blood taken, been given x-rays, and had another cat's paws touching her all over, including in places where only Topher should touch her. Lashonda didn't know what the two nurses had in mind for her next, but she was running out of patience. She hadn't even met Dr. Flockhart yet, let alone learned the deep, dark secret of her research.

Lashonda was beginning to wonder whether Dr. Flockhart was merely a front-name for a strange cult run by the Howards. Perhaps Vienne's father was against interspecies marriage and used these offices and his daughter to lure in couples before sticking them in cryo-tubes and shipping them off to work in secret sweatshops underneath the attractions on Moonville Funpark.

Lashonda's ears splayed in annoyance. "I didn't know the appointment would take this long," she grumbled, twitching her tail and feeling it tap against the white paper. "Besides, I'm not sure I'd feel comfortable eating lunch right now, all trussed up in this ridiculous paper."

"I'd feel a lot *more* comfortable eating lunch right now," Topher said.

Lashonda glared at him.

"What? I'm hungry. Besides, all that paper you're wearing would mean you wouldn't need any napkins. It's like you're dressed in a giant napkin."

Lashonda rolled her eyes. She didn't know how long they'd been waiting. Doctor's offices never seemed to have clocks; they existed in that in-between time where you wait and wait, minutes and hours interchangeable.

"I wonder what kind of restaurants they have on this island," Topher said. "Some of those cafes we passed looked promising. Maybe we'll finally get to try out otter cuisine."

Lashonda knew he was trying to ease the discomfort of waiting by striking up a conversation, but she couldn't bring herself to play her part. Topher began to brainstorm joke ideas to his non-responsive wife, and Lashonda silently fell deeper and deeper into her conspiracy theories involving the Howards until the black cat nurse finally returned.

"Thank you for your patience," the nurse said. "Dr. Flockhart can see you now."

In the doorway, behind the black cat nurse, stood an Australian Shepherd wearing a long white jacket and holding a medical chart in her paws. Her face was mottled black-white-and-grey with longer tufts of fur around her triangular ears, slightly flopped at their tips, and she had startling blue eyes.

The nurse left and shut the door behind her, leaving them alone with Dr. Flockhart.

"I'll be brief," the doctor said.

Lashonda swallowed her impulse to reply with sarcasm.

The doctor continued. "Your test results show that the two of you are compatible both with each other and with the program I'm running."

"With each other?" Topher asked. "Who else would we be compatible with?"

Dr. Flockhart smiled thinly, as if Topher had made a poor joke and she was humoring him. "Obviously, I can't pick individuals and match them purely on their genetic compatibility." Though her tone suggested that was exactly what she wanted to do. "I have to work with pre-existing couples who already want to have children together. That said, some genetic pairs are much better matched than others, and my techniques are still very new. So, I have to pick couples who have a high probability of being a good genetic match."

"How new?" Topher asked.

Lashonda felt a strange thrill, realizing that Dr. Flockhart had just told her that she and Topher were a good genetic match. The words sounded coldly scientific, but the concept was heartening. It felt like a strange sort of validation for their relationship.

Again, Dr. Flockhart ignored Topher's question. "Some breeds of dog seem to have genes that are much harder to combine with feline genes than other breeds. You're the first pug we've seen." Finally, Dr. Flockhart turned to look at Topher, but Lashonda couldn't help thinking that she was looking at him more like she would look at a lab experiment than a person. Topher shifted uncomfortably under her gaze.

Lashonda broke the awkward silence. "Are you saying what it sounds like you're saying?" The insides of her ears burned red with embarrassment as she forced herself to ask the ridiculous: "You can help us have children? Me and Topher—a cat and a dog—together? *Hybrids?*" Her tongue tripped over the final word, trying to stop her from making a fool of herself.

Dr. Flockhart's answer was simple. "Yes."

Lashonda didn't know what to say, and, from the silence that rang through the small examining room, she guessed Topher didn't either.

"I think there's a good probability of success here," Dr. Flockhart said. "If you'd like to proceed, we can set up an appointment for the next time you're in heat, Lashonda. Topher can set up his appointment for the same time."

Lashonda's ears rang with echoes of Dr. Flockhart's words. They were impossible and matter-of-fact at the same time. She couldn't reconcile the fantastical suggestion that she and Topher could have children together spoken side by side with the pedestrian idea of scheduling appointments.

"After I gather gametes from each of you," Dr. Flockhart continued, "it'll take me a couple of months to craft a selection of viable embryos for implantation. Lashonda, you'll need to take a special hormone treatment for several weeks before the implantation to get your body ready. That will involve several additional appointments. So, are you on board?"

Dr. Flockhart flashed them the cheerful grin of a herd dog who had her flock in order. Clearly, she knew what answer Topher and Lashonda had to give. What other answer could they give? It was as if an actual human had traveled forward through time and promised to grant their fondest wish using the secrets of the lost genetic sciences that had uplifted cats and dogs in the first place.

"How have we not heard about this before?" Topher asked.

Lashonda wanted to unsheathe her claws and swat him on the nose. How dare he say anything that might risk Dr. Flockhart's willingness to work with them? She held her breath, waiting for the doctor's answer.

Dr. Flockhart's cheerful grin faded to a gentle smile. "Do you think that the two of you would have ever made it this far into my program if my background checks hadn't suggested I could trust you completely to keep the secret of what we're doing here?"

Topher's small, flopped ears shifted slightly on his head, indicating his surprise at her answer.

"You will keep this secret." The way Dr. Flockhart said it, it wasn't a question, but it raised questions.

If Dr. Flockhart could keep her work secret, could she also keep success secret? Were there already cat-dog hybrids passing for normal cats and dogs? Or living among otters, away from the more conservative, dog-run nations? If she looked hard enough on Friedan Isle, Lashonda wondered, could she find them? Though, Dr. Flockhart said her techniques were still new. Perhaps all the hybrids were still babies. How many of them were there?

Impulsively, Lashonda said, "We're in." Then her ears flatted in sudden embarrassment for having answered a question she had no right—or ability—to answer alone. She looked at Topher.

"Don't look at me," he said. "You're the one who will need hormone treatments and will have to be pregnant. If you say we're in, we're in."

"Great!" Dr. Flockhart said. "Check in with Kevin on your way out, and he'll set up your next appointment. See you in a few weeks!" She spoke with an air of finality, and, before Lashonda could think of anything else to say, Dr. Flockhart opened the door, stepped through, and closed it behind her.

It took a few moments for it to sink in that their appointment was over, and Lashonda could get dressed again. They could talk to Kevin, set up an appointment, and return to their normal lives. Except, normal wasn't normal anymore. Now Lashonda lived in a world where cats and dogs could breed together; a world where she could expect to be a mother. Yet, everything felt the same, eerily the same as it all had before, even though she'd learned something that made everything different.

Topher picked up her clothes and handed them to her. "Let's get out of here and try one of those cafes."

They spent the rest of the afternoon enjoying Friedan Isle.

They ate trout chowder at a sidewalk cafe under a blue parasol, and Topher found a sweets shop where he bought candied clam chews and starfish taffy. They strolled, paw in paw, along the walkways beside the rivulets, bathed in the golden glow from the solar paneled buildings. All the while they discussed names for their future litter and imagined exactly what a pug-faced black kitten or feline puppy with green eyes would look like.

CHAPTER 8

Lashonda's next several appointments with Dr. Flockhart's office could have been perfectly normal doctor appointments except that she had to take a ferry to Friedan Isle for them. At the first one, the black cat nurse, named Nellie, measured Lashonda's weight and blood pressure, took a blood sample, and then assisted Dr. Flockhart in performing an ultrasound. Next, they sedated her for a brief, twenty minute operation. When she woke up, Nellie told her the appointment was over.

She found Topher in the waiting room, talking to Vienne Howard's husband.

The next series of appointments were all similar except less intrusive. Lashonda was, thankfully, allowed to skip the paper gown. Nellie measured her weight and blood pressure, then gave her an injection. Lashonda didn't even see Dr. Flockhart.

After each appointment, Topher and Lashonda repeated their afternoon of strolling through Friedan Isle and dining at the sidewalk cafe with the blue parasols. Even though Topher wasn't technically necessary for Lashonda's appointments, he came along anyway. He didn't want to miss a moment of the miracle that was the creation of their impossible litter. The more excited

Topher became, the more nervous Lashonda felt. She wanted to confide in Kelly, but she hadn't even told her sisters that they were trying to adopt. Jumping straight from "I never want to have a litter" to "I'm going to let a mad scientist make me pregnant with genetically engineered cat-dog hybrids" was too much.

When Nellie gave Lashonda her last injection of hormones, she said, "For your next appointment, we'll need you to stay several days. Dr. Flockhart has to monitor you to make sure the embryos implant properly in your uterus."

"How many days?" Lashonda asked, getting down from the examining table.

"That depends on how quickly the embryos implant," Nellie said. "You should plan on staying a week, but it'll probably be two or three days."

Topher put an arm around Lashonda, possessively. "Can I stay with her?"

Nellie smiled sympathetically. Her expression made it clear the answer was *no*. "Sorry. We only have space for patients here, but you can visit during the day."

Topher squeezed Lashonda's shoulder. "I'll come visit every day."

"You can't take that much time off from work," Lashonda said. "You know that. But we can talk on the phone every night." Turning to Nellie, she asked, "How soon?"

"Tell Kevin that we need you back in one week."

In the waiting room, they ran into Vienne Howard's husband again. Lashonda stepped up to the front desk to arrange her next appointment with Kevin; meanwhile, Topher and the orange tom cat chatted. Lashonda watched them out of the corner of her eye.

Kevin gave Lashonda a slip of paper with a reminder to bring an overnight bag to her appointment the following week. She thanked him, feeling distracted by the friendliness she could see in the orange tom's demeanor. He'd really warmed up to Topher.

"Okay," Lashonda said, interrupting them. "I'm ready. Let's go to lunch."

"Actually," Topher said, "I was just telling Rick about the place we usually eat, and we thought it would be fun to all go out for lunch together."

"Yeah," Rick said. "Vienne should be done with her appointment in a few minutes, if you don't mind waiting."

Lashonda did mind waiting, and the tip of her tail twitched impatiently. Topher saw her hesitation and stepped closer to her, turning his body away from Rick so they could confer quietly, privately. "You've said that you could use someone to talk to—someone who understands what you're going through."

The twitch in Lashonda's tail grew to an unhappy swish.

"Oh, come on," Topher said. "Give Vienne a chance. Her husband is really nice, so she can't be all bad. Besides, if anyone knows that public and private personas don't necessarily match, it should be the cat married to Topher Brooke."

Lashonda frowned, but she said, "All right. We can have lunch with them."

They didn't have to wait, after all. Vienne came out before Lashonda had a chance to sit down on one of the waiting room chairs. She wore a sundress patterned with giant pink flowers and a mauve knit sweater. *Did she always wear pink?*, Lashonda wondered.

Vienne saw her husband with Topher and Lashonda, and the ruffled skirt of her dress began to twitch with the wagging tip of her tail. Rick told her that they were all going to lunch together, and Vienne's tail wagged even more furiously. For a moment, Lashonda thought Vienne would break into high-pitched yipping about how excited she was. Instead, Vienne locked eyes with Lashonda and simply said, in a steady voice, "That sounds really nice."

Lashonda felt a strange relief, and the fur on her shoulders, which she hadn't even realized had been raised, began to smooth down again. Often times, dogs showed more emotion than most cats were comfortable with. Perhaps Lashonda shouldn't have been surprised that Vienne knew how to handle cats, being married to a tom, but Lashonda hadn't expected a small breed dog who always wore garish, pink dresses to show an even-keeled self-control.

The two couples walked along the pathways beside the city's rivulets, over arched footbridges, and through a tunnel through the base of one of the golden buildings to get to the Beachcomber Cafe. As they walked, Rick asked Topher questions about his job, displaying true curiosity about the career of a comedian.

Vienne and Lashonda walked together quietly, and, again, Lashonda was relieved and surprised that this strange dog who seemed so desperately to want to befriend her didn't take the opportunity to bark her head off. Instead, she walked silently beside Lashonda, listening to Topher talk. The only thing she said before they reached the cafe was, "Look," while pointing toward the rivulet where a pair of otters, dressed in serious business suits, bobbed in the water, splashing each other like pups.

Lashonda smiled. She still found it funny to see otters with their long spines, short legs, wide tails, and small ears jumping in and out of the rivulets like it was a perfectly normal way to travel. A few dogs, who mostly looked like Labradors, followed suit, but Lashonda didn't see any of the cats of Friedan Isle swimming.

They arrived at the Beachcomber Cafe, and a tabby cat waiter in Bermuda shorts and a Hawaiian shirt seated them under one of the blue parasols. He recommended the trout chowder, as it was the cafe's specialty. All of them ordered it except Topher who planned to work his way through the cafe's whole menu. Today, he'd worked his way up to the red snapper.

While they waited, Rick kept asking Topher questions like, "Where do you get ideas for your jokes?" Topher ate up the attention, clearly happy as a clam; he could talk about writing jokes for hours. The story of each joke became a heroic journey he'd made to craft the perfect set up, find the perfect punch line, and execute the perfect delivery.

Vienne smiled politely, but her eyes gazed dully past Topher at the view of the otters swimming and small boats drifting along the rivulet. Occasionally, she glanced at Lashonda and her muzzle broke into a smile. Then, she'd look back at the rivulet.

"Would you swim in there?" Lashonda asked, finally feeling comfortable with Vienne.

"I'm not much of a swimmer. What about you?"

Lashonda waited a moment, expecting Vienne to make a joke about cats and water. Heaven knew that Topher had an entire routine of them, though that was part of his stage persona. It was different when dogs made jokes like that, forcing cats into pigeonholes, in real life. It was different when they meant them.

Lashonda waited, but Vienne didn't tell a joke. She really meant her question.

"Maybe," Lashonda said.

Vienne lifted her pink-dyed eyebrows, but she didn't say anything.

"I always wanted to be an otter when I was a kitten," Lashonda said, feeling safe enough to explain herself. "Though, I'd probably want a towel, and I don't think I'd like to get my clothes wet."

"I'd feel weird about how these canals are really part of the ocean," Vienne said. "How deep do they go? If I sank, would I sink all the way down?" She shuddered. "No, I'd rather swim at a water park. Lots of slides and rides."

"Like Moonville Funpark," Lashonda said, before she could stop herself. "I'm sorry." She'd just done to Vienne what she'd been afraid Vienne would do to her: stereotype her based on the only thing she knew about her—her father's estate. "Everyone must bring up Moonville Funpark to you."

"It's okay," Vienne said. "Have you ever been there?"

"Topher and I wanted to go to the otter space station and visit Moonville Funpark for our honeymoon, but we couldn't afford it." Lashonda felt weird admitting to money concerns while talking to one of the richest dogs on the planet. Fortunately, it was easy to change the subject. "How have your appointments with Dr. Flockhart been going?"

And, suddenly, Vienne's muzzle split into a grin bright enough to outshine the sun. She looked down embarrassed, and, when she looked back up, she said, "I'm a month along. Dr. Flockhart says that three of the embryos took." She reached under the table and grabbed Rick's paw. "We're having a litter of three!"

"Wow," Lashonda breathed. The reality of her own, impending appointment weighed heavily on her, and she struggled not to hyperventilate. "Have you told any of your family?"

Vienne laughed. "My mom is convinced that I'm having an affair with Josh. You know, the yellow Labrador nurse? And that Rick's too stupid to realize it. Honestly, I think my parents are so deluded and self-involved that when I show them my kittens, they'll just think they're slightly funny-looking Chihuahua puppies."

Lashonda wondered whether half-pug kittens could pass for half-Persian instead. That might explain flat faces, but it wouldn't explain corkscrew tails or flopped ears. Again,

Lashonda wondered if there were already cat-dog hybrids out in the world. If she'd ever met one, would she even know?

"I wish," she said, "that we could meet some of the litters Dr. Flockhart's already delivered. I keep hoping I'll cross paths with one of the successful mothers in the waiting room."

Vienne tilted her head and narrowed her eyes quizzically. "Don't you know?" she asked.

"Know what?"

Vienne leaned back in her chair and placed her paws protectively on her still-flat belly, covered by pink-flower print. "You'll have to wait several months for that."

Lashonda blinked. "Do you mean..."

Vienne took a nervous sip of her water and then said, "There's a cat married to a West Highland Terrier who's two months ahead of me, but that's the farthest anyone's gotten."

Those words didn't sit well with Lashonda. Her ears splayed to the sides. "What do you mean 'the farthest anyone's gotten?'"

The table had gotten quiet. Lashonda looked at Topher and saw he'd stopped talking to Rick. Vienne fidgeted uncomfortably, turning her water glass round and round in her paws; her ears splayed to the sides as well. For a dog, she was awfully cat-like.

Rick glanced at his wife. He started to speak, but then he saw the waiter-cat coming their way, balancing a tray bearing three steaming bowls and a plate of red snapper. The waiter greeted them cheerfully and passed out their meals. He left with the tray tucked under his arm, and Rick watched him go.

Once the waiter was out of ear shot, Rick said, "From what I've gathered, most couples don't get invited back after their initial two visits. Dr. Flockhart isn't even able to make a viable slate of embryos for them. Then, there are the couples where the embryos don't take."

Lashonda blinked in surprise. She'd spent so much time

planning for adoption and so little time thinking about pregnancy. It hadn't occurred to her that her appointment next week wouldn't necessarily result in a pregnancy let alone a litter.

Rick's voice got low, and he said, "We also know there's been at least one miscarriage." He looked at Vienne.

"Jenny," Vienne said, staring numbly at her bowl of chowder.

"Right," Rick agreed. "She was a Papillon married to a tabby tom. They started the program at the same time we did."

"I thought we were becoming friends," Vienne said. "We talked about having our litters play together. She won't talk to me any more."

Rick put an orange-striped paw on Vienne's shoulder. "It probably hurts too much, honey."

"Yeah, I know." Vienne picked up a spoon and stirred her chowder idly. "I probably wouldn't talk to her either, if our situations were reversed. In fact, I think I'm more bothered by imagining how easily it could have been me than by losing her friendship. I guess, if we miscarry too,"—her voice caught on the word 'miscarry,' and she put down her spoon—"then, she'll probably talk to me. At least, I'd have a friend who'd understand." She laughed bitterly. "Shared misery. Small consolation."

From the tension in the air, Lashonda could tell that a miscarriage must be a big deal, but she felt like she was missing something. "Can't she try again?" Lashonda asked. "Couldn't you try again? If you—" She didn't want to say 'miscarry' after seeing how the word affected Vienne. "I mean..."

"No," Rick said. Cold and final. His tone of voice did not invite the question 'why?'

Topher asked anyway.

Rick glared at him.

"It's all right," Vienne said to Rick. "It's better to talk about it. I can't hold my breath for the next seven months, and neither can you."

Rick's ears flattened; he looked abashed. The orange tomcat and his Chihuahua wife stared at each other, exchanging meaning with their eyes that no one outside their marriage could guess at or understand. He turned back to Topher and said, "Dr. Flockhart only wants to spend her time on the couples most likely to succeed. She told Jenny that the miscarriage was a sign that she and her husband weren't the best genetic match. You get one shot. That's it."

No one knew what to say to that, and, for a while, the two couples ate their meal in silence.

A group of otters at a neighboring table finished their meal and paid the waiter-cat. They walked together, talking, to the edge of the wide walkway beside the cafe's tables. One of them said, loudly enough to be heard at Lashonda's table, "Should we wait for a boat?"

"I don't see any reason to," another otter answered.

Then, one by one, the otters dove off the edge.

Vienne laughed, and Lashonda smiled. But Rick's ears were still flat; they had been for a while, and a few otters diving fully clothed into the rivulet wasn't enough to straighten them.

"Otters," Topher said, shaking his jowly head.

The tip of Lashonda's tail twitched expectantly. She knew the tone of Topher's voice when he was about to tell a joke. "Yeah, *otters*," she said, cajoling him to go on. With all the interest Rick had shown in Topher's job, a joke might actually cheer him up. And she wasn't sure she could stand this much tension through the rest of their lunch. She had enough to be stressed out about without an unhappy tomcat broadcasting his emotions at her.

"Hey, Rick," Topher said. "How many otters does it take to change a light bulb?"

Rick's ears perked up, and his whiskers straightened. He put his spoon down in his bowl of chowder and pushed the bowl forward slightly. He intended to enjoy his moment with a professional comedian to the fullest. "How many?"

"Three," Topher said.

Lashonda hoped Rick wouldn't be disappointed. She knew this joke; it was from Topher's file of 'social jokes'—ones that weren't good enough to use in his routines but could be thrown around on social occasions.

"Why three?" Rick asked. His eyes shone like a kitten's who'd been picked to help the clown make balloon animals at a birthday party. Hopefully, he'd keep his claws sheathed and not pop the balloon.

"Two to set up the water slide," Topher said. "And one to hire a dog to change the light bulb."

Rick laughed, and everyone relaxed.

They stuck to small talk through the rest of their lunch. When the waiter-cat brought out a dessert menu, Topher ordered a basket of candied clams for everyone to share. After that, Vienne suggested they try out one of the boat rides. So, they hired an otter with a small boat to ferry them around the isle. He pointed out the sights while Topher cracked jokes and Rick ate them up. By the end of the afternoon, Lashonda actually hoped that she and Topher would run into Vienne and Rick again.

On the ferry home, Lashonda watched the sunset shine on the water, orange and pink, and she listened to the seagulls squalling. She wanted to talk to Topher about what they'd learned—that they'd only have one chance at a family, and it might not take. But she couldn't bring herself to say the words, any words, and he didn't say them either.

Yet, when one of the seagulls swooped by and snatched a bagel from the paws of an unwitting kitten, who proceeded to squeal with an emotion somewhere between outrage and amusement, Topher caught Lashonda's eye. He smiled, turning up the folds of his jowly face, but there was a touch of sadness, perhaps wistfulness in the expression.

"Everything will work out," Topher said. "One way or the other."

Lashonda nodded.

"Do you want to talk about it?" he asked. "You know, what Rick said." Topher's jowls had set into a determined expression; a look he got when he was trying to hold back his feelings.

Lashonda still couldn't bring herself to say anything. There were too many feelings, and they were too complex for words.

"Maybe it's best if we... don't talk about it?" Topher sounded hopeful. He didn't want to talk about it either.

Lashonda nodded, more vigorously this time. "Talking wouldn't change anything," she said. "And like you say, it'll work out. Somehow."

Topher took Lashonda's paw and squeezed it. They were on a ferry together at sunset. It was a beautiful moment and didn't need words. Nonetheless, the uncertainty of Lashonda's next appointment hung over them, the subject of their silence as much as anything can be a subject of conversation.

CHAPTER 9

Along week later, Lashonda and Topher took the early morning train to the docks and then the ferry across the water to Friedan Isle again. The world slipped past Lashonda in tunnels of gray, sheets of blue, and finally jumbles of gold. Nothing felt real to her.

The trip had grown routine, nearly mundane, but it was different this time. She wouldn't be coming home until she was pregnant or, else, knew she never would be.

Topher carried Lashonda's suitcase and held her paw as they walked along the rivulets of Friedan Isle to the building that housed Dr. Flockhart's offices. They didn't talk, but the purpose of Lashonda's appointment hung over them anyway.

Inside Dr. Flockhart's building, they waited for the elevator. As the lights above the elevator counted down through the floors showing the elevator's approach, Topher said, "If this doesn't work, I want to take you on a trip to Deep Sky Anchor and Moonville Funpark. Okay? It'll be the honeymoon we couldn't afford when we got married."

"What if this does work?" Lashonda asked. She kept trying to imagine how she'd feel if the embryos took. If they didn't take, nothing would change—nothing would ever change. She and Topher would not have a litter, never raise children. She'd be devastated. Did that mean she'd feel ecstatic if the embryos did take? Or just not devastated? She wasn't sure. She couldn't push her mind through the veil of time and pre-experience her emotions.

The elevator arrived at their floor, and the doors opened.

"If it does work," Topher said, stepping into the elevator, "then you'll be carrying my litter and won't belong on any crazy Funpark rides. It wouldn't be safe."

Lashonda felt a glow at Topher's words, and the feeling gave her hope. Maybe she would be ecstatic if the embryos took. She wished she could be sure. She followed Topher inside the elevator and took his paw. She said, "I hope we don't get to go on the trip."

The elevator doors closed behind them.

Topher put her suitcase down on the floor of the elevator and wrapped his arms around her. "Me too," he said.

She leaned her head against him, and her whiskers smashed against the comforting bulk of his barrel chest. A purr rumbled deep in her throat.

When the elevator doors opened, they stepped awkwardly apart, strangely embarrassed to have Kevin see them cuddling, despite the purpose of Lashonda's visit.

The deeply intimate was depersonalized here. In the next few days, Lashonda's body would be invaded and altered in ways that usually happened in the privacy of night in one's own bedroom under the soft touch of a lover. Instead, Lashonda's beloved would be miles away, back on the mainland. She would be here with the nurses, Nelly and Josh, and the ever-elusive, cold and clinical Dr. Flockhart. She'd be touched by needles and latex gloves instead of warm, loving paws.

"What will you do while I'm gone?" Lashonda asked, stepping out of the elevator.

Topher waited to answer her question while Lashonda

checked in with Kevin. Once they were seated in the small waiting area, he said, "I thought I'd use your synthesizer to build an army of robots that look exactly like me. Then we'll take over the city."

Lashonda dipped one ear and stared at him through skeptical eyes. "My machine doesn't work that way."

"No?" he said. "Well, maybe I'll just make one robot that looks like you, because I'll miss you so much."

"If you're lucky," Lashonda said, "you could maybe coax my synthesizer into printing a tiny statuette of me."

"Hmm. You're ruining all my plans."

Lashonda's emerald eyes laughed.

"Okay," Topher said, "then, I'll pretend that I invented your machine, sell it to the otters, and go become a mad scientist on Deep Sky Anchor."

Lashonda twisted her other ear around. "Well, at least that's more likely than your other suggestions. You should probably leave my synthesizer alone though."

"That would be easier," he countered, "if you didn't have pieces of it spread out all over the floor. I'll be tripping over it all week."

The black cat nurse, Nelly, poked her head through the door into the waiting area. "Lashonda? We're ready for you."

Lashonda stood up and grabbed her suitcase. "Just imagine," she said to Topher, "that I left my synthesizer all spread out so that every time you tripped, it would remind you of me."

Topher took the suitcase from her paws, set it back down on the floor, and then swept Lashonda into a passionate embrace. His kiss left her whiskers tingling. "Okay, you can have her now," he said to Nelly. "But if you don't take good care of her, I'll be back with an army of robots to exact revenge."

Lashonda said goodbye to her husband, and the two black cats, nurse and patient, disappeared into the inner offices, leaving Topher to his own devices for the week. Lashonda suspected he'd camp out on the sofa in the Nightly Howl writers' den and pick up junk food from sidewalk food carts for his meals all week. She knew he would call her every day.

Nelly brought Lashonda to a small room decorated with yellow fake flowers and blue curtains. It held a small bed, a single rocking chair, a sink with a mirror behind it, and a door to a small bathroom.

"This is where I'll be staying?" Lashonda asked.

"Yes. You can leave your suitcase here. Please change into the gown laid out on your bed. We'll be ready for your implantation surgery in about ten minutes." Nelly dipped her ears and straightened them again in a subtle gesture of deference.

Lashonda felt her own ears mimic the gesture. It always felt eerie to her to interact with another black cat. She had been the only solid black kitten in her litter, and her education and career choices had led to her spending a great deal of time with dogs, so it didn't happen all that often. The place she saw black cats most often was in her own mirror.

Nelly closed the door behind her, leaving Lashonda alone with a hospital gown. At least it was cloth this time. Instead of plain white like the paper gowns, this one was covered in tiny, purple flowers. Lashonda put it on. Then she carefully folded her own clothes and put them away in her suitcase. She didn't think she'd need them again until it was time to go home. Most doctors seemed to prefer their patients in hospital gowns whenever possible, so she suspected she'd be wearing this one for the rest of her visit.

Lashonda sat on the bed, her tail twitching, and waited. After a few minutes, she started taking the things out of her suitcase and arranged them around the room. She placed a framed picture of Topher on the windowsill beside her bed. She laid out her brush, toothbrush, and toothpaste on the counter by the sink. When she pulled the alarm clock she'd brought to combat the timelessness of Dr. Flockhart's office out of her suitcase, her whiskers turned down into a frown. Based on when she'd arrived, she guessed that she'd been waiting in this room for nearly half an hour, well longer than the ten minutes Nelly promised.

Lashonda scuffed her claws on the floor. She'd be in this room for days, so it shouldn't matter that her surgery was running late. Still, the sooner they started, the sooner it would all be over.

As she thought that, Lashonda realized she didn't expect the surgery to work. She picked up the picture of Topher and narrowed her eyes, examining every detail of his goofy, canine smile—the wrinkly folds of fur on his brow and around his muzzle; the flop of his dark brown ears; and the soft brown of his eyes, completely different from cat eyes.

One thing she'd known since the end of her kittenhood was that a dog could not make her pregnant. She never needed to fear growing heavy with a life-changing litter from a dog. But, now, a mad dog scientist promised to change that unalterable fact and make her pregnant with Topher's litter. Clearly, it was impossible.

Although, Vienne claimed to be carrying Rick's litter. Lashonda's ears flattened. Maybe it was possible.

She heard noise outside her door, the scuffling of paws, muffled voices, and then hysterical sobs. The sobbing voice sounded like Vienne's. Lashonda opened the door and poked her head out. She saw Josh, the Labrador nurse, blocking Rick's way.

"You can't come back here," Josh said. "Please, go back to the waiting room."

"I need to be with my wife!" Rick yowled.

"Rick?" Lashonda said.

His orange-striped head turned her way. His green eyes were wild and frantic; the fur around his face bushed out.

"What's going on?" Lashonda asked. She felt self-conscious

in her hospital gown, but she stepped out into the hall anyway.

Rick's fur smoothed down as he looked at her. "They've taken Vienne back there, and they won't let me go with her."

"I didn't know you had an appointment today," Lashonda said.

"We didn't," Rick stammered.

"So, why are you here? I didn't see you on the ferry ride over."

Rick took a step toward Lashonda, and she opened the door to her room wider, gesturing for him to follow her inside. Standing behind Rick, Josh mouthed the words, "Thank you." Now that Rick was calming down, Josh began backing away, toward the surgery room they must have taken Vienne into.

Lashonda sat down on her bed and gestured for Rick to sit in the rocking chair. As soon as he sat, he grabbed the tip of his tail with his paws and started rocking nervously. "Vienne spent the whole ferry ride in the bathroom crying," he said. "That's why you didn't see us. I didn't know what to do, so I just stood there, listening and waiting for her."

"Why was she crying?" Lashonda asked, a sense of horror growing in the pit of her stomach.

"She was bleeding," Rick said. "She started bleeding last night, and she says she feels *wrong*. She's worried about the babies."

Lashonda held her arms wide, offering a hug, and Rick didn't hesitate. He jumped out of the rocking chair and curled up against her, starting to sob, himself. Lashonda stroked the back of his head, smoothing his bushy fur, and mewed soothing words as he cried into her shoulder. The clock ticked through an hour that way.

Finally, Josh came to the door and said, "Rick, you can come see Vienne now. And, Lashonda, we're sorry you've had to wait so long. We'll be ready for your implantation surgery in another ten minutes."

"What happened?" Rick asked, wiping his paws against his eyes, trying to dry the fur on his face. He wouldn't want Vienne to see he'd been crying. He'd want to be strong for her. "Did we lose the litter?" His whiskers only trembled a little as he said it.

Josh glanced at Lashonda as if wondering whether it was all right to talk about Vienne's condition in front of her, but he must have decided it was okay. "You only lost one of the fetuses," Josh said. "One of them had died. If we hadn't surgically removed it, her body might have rejected the whole litter shortly. It's good that you came in when you did."

Rick had been standing up, but he literally staggered back against the bed at Josh's news. "You mean—we still have a litter?"

Josh nodded solemnly in confirmation. "Yes, a litter of two."

Rick pushed himself up from the bed, straightened out his clothes, and tried to regain the dignity he'd shed while sobbing. "Okay, take me to Vienne," he said. Then, as he followed Josh out the door, he looked back at Lashonda and dipped his ears. He was too proud to thank her directly—that would acknowledge his breakdown—but he didn't need to say the words for her to understand.

Lashonda wondered how Topher would handle it if the two of them ended up back here, losing members of their unborn litter one by one. He'd be strong for her, but would he break down in tears when she was out of sight? Maybe it would be better if the embryos didn't take. Then the heartbreak would be over all at once.

"Lashonda?" Nelly said, standing in the doorway. Her green scrubs matched her eyes. Green is a good color on a black cat, much better than little purple flowers. "We're ready for you now. Come on." She held out a paw, indicating that Lashonda should get up and follow her.

The two black cats padded their way down the hall into an operating room, the purple-flowered hospital gown following the green scrubs. Nelly helped Lashonda onto an operating table and told her to lie down.

Lashonda stared at the wide, rectangular ceiling tiles and wished the implantation were already over.

Dr. Flockhart came into the room, wearing her long white coat. "Good afternoon, Lashonda," she said. "How are you feeling?"

"Fine," Lashonda lied, closing her eyes.

"Great. I've got ten embryos prepared for you."

Lashonda's eyes shot back open. "Ten?" she asked, trying to push herself up to see them, as if the sight of a few barely-multi-cellular embryos would show her what Topher's and her children would look like.

Nelly pushed her back down against the operating table.

"Yes, ten," Dr. Flockhart said. "I don't expect that many to take."

Restrained against the table, Lashonda said, "Only three of them took for Vienne. Did you prepare ten for her as well?"

Dr. Flockhart hesitated a moment and then said, "I always prepare ten."

Lashonda felt Dr. Flockhart's paws on her, pressing and poking against her belly, and shifted uncomfortably under the moving pressure. She closed her eyes again. The strangeness of the experience washed over her. She tried to imagine that the paws touching her were Topher's—that he was here with her instead. But this experience, lying on a hard operating table, invaded by medical tools and tubes, was more like going to the dentist than making a litter of puppies the traditional way. She counted the seconds until it was over.

"Okay, Lashonda," Dr. Flockhart said, signaling the end of the procedure. "You did great. Nelly will take you back to your room, and we'll check on you every couple hours to see how you're progressing."

Lashonda opened her eyes and got up from the table. She

passed her paws over the purple flower print covering her body. She didn't feel any different.

On the way back to her room, she and Nelly passed the room where Vienne was recovering. Lashonda could hear Rick inside. He mewed soothing words, urging Vienne to think of the two babies they had left. She could also hear Vienne—crying over the one they'd lost. His name was Jimathon.

Lashonda swore to herself that she wouldn't name any of her litter until she was holding them in her arms. But she knew it wasn't a promise she could keep. She was already wondering how many of the embryos would take—how many boys' names would she need? And how many girls'?

THE NEXT DAYS were the most agonizingly long days of Lashonda's life to date. The hours crawled by. She tried to work on her laptop, writing a paper about the discoveries she'd made building her home-sized synthesizer. If the dogs running the labs wouldn't look at her work directly, maybe they'd pay attention to publication credits, and she was sure she could get her work published. However, she couldn't concentrate and found herself mostly waiting for Josh or Nellie to come interrupt.

Every few hours, one of them wheeled in the portable ultrasound machine—Josh during the day, and Nellie in the evenings. Lashonda couldn't understand the monochrome squiggles on its greenish-black screen, but she could read the expression on Josh's face. The set of his jowls was serious; the angle of his brows concerned.

"Of course," he said, his face transforming to jovial jocularity, "we can't really tell from the ultrasound. We need the blood test."

Lashonda's arm ached. He'd taken so much of her blood.

Nellie's face was much harder to read. Her green eyes

narrowed at the screen, revealing nothing while scrutinizing everything. However, Nellie liked to talk, and Lashonda learned that she was much more than one of Dr. Flockhart's nurses. She was Dr. Flockhart's wife. The two of them lived in an apartment adjoining their medical offices.

Lashonda watched The Nightly Howl on her laptop each night and then waited for Topher to call. He didn't ask her if the embryos had taken. He didn't ask if she was pregnant. He only asked if she knew when she was coming home, and she had to say *no*. Each day, it seemed more likely that the answer to all his unasked questions would be *no*, too.

The fifth day, Dr. Flockhart came into Lashonda's room, muzzle beaming and tail wagging. "Congratulations!"

Lashonda's fur fluffed up all over her body. She could hardly believe this moment had come, and she didn't know how to react. Then she thought of Vienne's litter of three—now a litter of two. "How many?" she asked, hoping for as many as possible to increase the chances of some of them making it.

"Oh, we can't tell that yet," Dr. Flockhart said, the expression on her muzzle turning serious. "Now, I'll need you back in a month. That's when we'll do the ultrasound where we can finally count the number of embryos that implanted properly." Her tail continued to wag furiously under her lab coat. It was such a departure from her earlier demeanor. It couldn't help but inspire confidence. "If you have any symptoms that worry you, give us a call, and if you start bleeding—" The wag in her tail faltered, but it started up again. "Come in immediately."

And, like that, Lashonda's harrowing wait was over. She didn't feel ecstatic, but a peacefulness came over her. The long search was over. Her litter wasn't waiting for her in a cattery somewhere, sad and lonely, losing hope with each passing moment that she'd come for them. Her litter was inside her, too small to see and too small to count, but *growing* and safe.

"I need to call Topher," she said.

"Of course. Take all the time you need, just make sure to check in with Kevin on the way out and set up your next appointment."

"In one month," Lashonda confirmed.

"Yes, one month." Dr. Flockhart turned to leave, but then she turned back. "I just want to say again, congratulations!"

Lashonda got the strange feeling that Dr. Flockhart was congratulating herself—Lashonda's personal success was Dr. Flockhart's scientific success. Her ears flattened, and she felt more than ever like a mad scientist's experiment. Still, it felt good to have her doctor's attention focused on her. "Thank you," she said.

Dr. Flockhart nodded and closed the door behind her.

Lashonda got dressed in her own clothes before vid-calling Topher on her laptop, so he knew as soon as he saw her that something had changed.

"You're not wearing the nightgown," he said. "Are you coming home?" The resolution of the vid-call was lower than the resolution of The Nightly Howl, but Lashonda could see he looked excited, also apprehensive.

"Yes, I'm coming home today." She knew what he wanted to know, but every way she could think of to say it felt weird. Even thinking the words "I'm pregnant" made the insides of her ears flush red, and she flattened them to hide her embarrassment.

"Do I need to buy airline tickets to the space elevator?" Topher asked, his tone even. Clearly, he couldn't read her complex emotions.

"Oh, right, the trip to Moonville Funpark," Lashonda said, remembering his promise of a trip into space if the embryos didn't take. Her voice got small, and she said, "No... I think we should stay home."

Topher's jowly muzzle split into the biggest grin she'd seen since accepting his proposal of marriage.

"You're going to make a good father," she said.

"And you'll be the best mother! Now get off this call, and come home right away! I'll meet you at the docks."

The whole way back to the mainland, Lashonda's ears buzzed. She felt lightheaded with the weight of the change in her life. Topher met her at the docks with a big embrace, and the two of them walked through the city, holding paws and talking about the coming months, for hours.

Then life went back to normal.

THE ONLY MATERIAL change in their lives was that Lashonda slept longer every day, and Vienne started calling her weekly, begging to have the four of them get together for coffee, lunch, dinner, or whatever else Lashonda would agree to. For the first month, Lashonda put her off, claiming a tiredness that was all too true.

At her next appointment with Dr. Flockhart, Lashonda heard her babies' heartbeats. Topher squeezed her paw as they listened to a cacophony of drumbeats as if her belly was filled with tiny helicopters. Dr. Flockhart counted blips on the ultrasound screen and announced that six of the embryos had taken. More than with any previous couple.

On the ferry ride home, Topher started talking about names for their litter, and Lashonda didn't stop him. Whether they named the litter early or not, Lashonda realized she was already attached to them. She pressed her paws against her flat belly. She knew they were inside, but it wasn't the same as seeing those tiny blips on the ultrasound screen. She already couldn't wait for her next appointment. She missed hearing their tiny hearts beat.

CHAPTER 10

The next time Vienne called, Lashonda was happy to hear from her. She wanted someone to talk to who could understand what she was going through, and she hadn't figured out what to tell her sisters. Lashonda and Vienne agreed to go on a double date that night at a burger place in the city called Everything Bacon.

Rick and Vienne were already sitting across from each other in one of the red vinyl booths at the burger joint when Topher and Lashonda arrived. So, Lashonda scooted in next to Vienne, and Topher sat by Rick.

"The special here is a peanut butter bacon burger," Rick said.

"That sounds great!" Topher said.

The idea of any food, lately, made Lashonda feel sick. She looked at the plastic coated menu and decided she'd just order a double cream milkshake.

Their waitress, a curly-eared spaniel woman, came to take their orders. "Will this all be together?" she asked.

"No," Topher said, "separate checks, please."

"Great!" she woofed. "Let's start with the lovely feline couple."

"Ah, no," Topher said. "The lovely feline lady is with *me*. The Chihuahua lady is with the tom."

"Oh! I'm sorry," the spaniel waitress said, looking flustered. "But, you can understand my confusion."

Rick frowned. "Just bring me a peanut butter bacon burger."

"Same," said Topher.

"Can you make that with almond butter and turkey bacon?" Vienne asked.

The spaniel waitress, who'd looked stricken by her mistake, was overjoyed to have the chance to make it up to them. "Sure can!"

Lashonda ordered her double cream shake, and, after the waitress asked them all several times if there was anything else she could do for them, she left them in peace.

"It's better for the babies, you know," Vienne said in a hushed voice.

"What is?" Lashonda asked.

"Turkey bacon and almond butter. If I eat anything too rich, it gives me a tummy ache, and that can't be good for them."

"Why are you whispering?" Rick asked, ears sidewise.

Vienne looked all around until she spotted the waitress: she was occupied at another table, taking an order, so Vienne felt free to speak. "Well, since you guys made such a big deal about us being mixed-species couples to the waitress, I figure we shouldn't let on to her that both of us ladies are—" her voice fell to a hush again, "—*pregnant*."

Rick's ears flattened. "What are you going to do? Stop being seen with me in public entirely when you start to show?"

Vienne touched her belly. She could still pull off a strappy, little pink dress. Lashonda wondered how much longer that would last.

"Actually," Vienne said, "the waitress' mistake gave me an idea. It would still be a few months off, but Rick has been talking about how it would be nice to do normal things that couples do when they're having a litter—like go to birth classes!"

Rick's ears stayed flattened, showing his embarrassment. "I thought *you* would like it," he said to her.

Vienne reached across the table and patted his striped paws. "Right, I meant that. Anyway, what if we did them together? All four of us? That way it wouldn't draw attention to us."

"What, you mean... switch... partners?" Topher asked.

"Yes," Rick said. His ears were still flattened. "That's what she means."

Topher looked like he was about to explain how that idea made him uncomfortable on a number of levels, but Lashonda cut him off, saying simply, "We'll think about it." That way she could deal with the problem later. "We found out our litter size."

Vienne clapped her paws and bounced in her seat excitedly. Then, a dark look crossed her face. Everyone at the table could see she was thinking of the baby she'd lost. She started to stammer something incoherent about how the number you start with isn't always the number you end up with, but Rick interrupted.

"It's okay," he said. "You don't have to explain. Lashonda was there, remember?"

"Yeah, we already know," Lashonda said as gently as she could.

"Oh good." Vienne's voice was small, but she pulled herself back together quickly. "So what did you find out about your litter?"

Lashonda tried and failed to not sound smug as she said, "Six."

If Vienne were a cat, she would have sounded snitty when

she said, "Wow, you could really end up with your paws full." Instead, she sounded completely sincere.

"Good for you," Rick said, slapping Topher on the shoulder.

The waitress interrupted them with their peanut butter bacon burgers and Lashonda's shake. She even brought little cups of extra peanut butter for the burgers to make up for the earlier misunderstanding. Spaniels could be kind of needy, but they made good waiters.

They ate for a while in silence, then Vienne said, "Have you heard about Lois?"

Lashonda looked at Topher; he didn't show any more recognition of the name than she felt. "Who's Lois?" she asked.

"Lois is the cat married to the West Highland Terrier," Vienne said. "They were going to have the first hybrid litter." She poked at the basket of fries that had come with her burger. "Well, not anymore. Now we're going to be first."

"What do you mean?" Lashonda asked with a sense of foreboding.

Rick said, "Lois lost her litter. She made it to three months. Once you get past three months, apparently, miscarriages are a lot less likely."

"Aren't you at two months?" Lashonda asked Vienne, trying to gauge by the look of her still-flat belly how far along she could be.

"Yes," she said. She laughed nervously. "I'm trying not to worry about the next month. Stress is bad for the babies."

Lashonda chanted the number *six* in her head like a mantra. She'd already had better luck than any of the other couples in terms of how many embryos implanted. Maybe she'd also have better luck with how long they'd last. It was a horrible thought, but she could afford to lose one fetus a month for the dangerous first three months, and they'd still have a litter of three. In fact, she was already a month along. So, she could even lose two per month and still come out of this with a litter.

Though, her heart ached at the thought of losing any of those six tiny blips with their helicopter-like heartbeats.

For the rest of their meal, the couples talked amiably. Lashonda confided how strange it was to be keeping this secret from her sisters. Vienne confessed her fear that her family's first real knowledge of her litter would come from the tabloids, whenever they inevitably found out. Topher and Rick talked about their fathers and fatherhood.

They had all the normal conversations that were otherwise denied them by their extraordinary circumstances. A normal couple could tell their waitress—or the checkout clerk at the grocery store, or anyone really—that they're expecting a litter and enjoy the small talk that made it all feel real. *"You must be so excited!" "Have you picked out any names?" "Are you hoping for a big litter or a small one?"* But Topher and Lashonda had experienced none of that until this conversation with Rick and Vienne.

When the couples said goodbye, they all knew they'd be getting together again soon. They all needed it.

OVER THE NEXT MONTH, the two couples spent an increasing amount of time together. When Vienne passed the three month mark in her pregnancy, she and Rick invited Lashonda and Topher to join them for dinner at a fancy rooftop restaurant to celebrate. That's when the media noticed Vienne Howard, heiress, and Topher Brooke, comedian, "out on the town together," in the words of the paparazzi who snapped their picture. No one seemed to notice the ginger tom and black lady cat in the picture with them. Sometimes, being a cat was a lot like being invisible.

Topher got permission from Vienne to play up their faux-romance on The Nightly Howl. A few weeks later, the tabloids' splashy news about "the whirlwind romance of the heiress and the comedian" made its way across the country to Lashonda's sisters on the other coast.

Kelly called concerned. After a few minutes of small talk while her orange-and-black ears flicked nervously, she said, "Okay, so what's the deal with Vienne Howard? Adelle says Topher's probably cheating on you, but I told her that he would never do that. Sherri thinks you're in on it, and he's trying to sweet talk his way into a Howard sponsored TV show of his own. We have a bet on it. So, what is it? Why is Topher all over the news with that trampy Chihuahua?"

"She's not trampy." Lashonda defended her friend, buying herself time to think. "Though, she does like pink too much."

"That is so not an answer." Kelly rolled her golden eyes.

Lashonda had expected to hear from her sisters about the "heiress and the comedian" scandal. She and Topher had talked about how to deal with it, and, at the time, she'd agreed with him that they should keep the secret of their impending litter from their families for as long as possible. However, seeing her sister's face on the vid-screen, she felt sorely tempted to tell her all about Dr. Flockhart and the hybrid litters that she and Vienne were carrying.

"What are you hiding?" Kelly asked, one ear skewed off to the side. "If Adelle was right, you'd be crying by now. If it was Sherri who's right, you'd be filling me in on the details of your clever scheme. So, I clearly won the bet, but something has to be going on."

Lashonda narrowed her green eyes, and, on the vid-screen, Kelly narrowed her golden eyes back at her. Kelly would keep her secret. Lashonda was sure of it. "Vienne and I have something in common," she said. "We met through our doctor."

"Oh, god, you don't have cancer, do you?" Kelly's ears flattened. "Surely it would be all over the news if Vienne Howard had cancer."

"No," Lashonda said. "I'm perfectly healthy. It's more... *out there* than that. This doctor is kind of experimental."

Kelly's ears straightened up, and her eyes glinted with amusement. "You're being transformed into a dog, aren't you? Gene therapy, crazy science stuff?"

Lashonda's whiskers twitched; she tried to imagine herself as a dog and failed. An otter, maybe. But not a dog. "You're half right," she said. "It is gene therapy and crazy science stuff."

This time Kelly waited for Lashonda to continue. There were no more guesses to delay the big announcement.

"Topher and I are having a litter."

Kelly blinked, but she didn't say anything. Neither did Lashonda.

"A litter of what?" Kelly asked.

Lashonda's ears flattened. "Kittens? Puppies? I don't know what to call them, but I'm almost three months along. And so far, it looks like a litter of six."

"Wow."

Lashonda didn't think Kelly's eyes could get any wider. "You can't tell anyone," she said. "Not Adelle or Sherri. Not even Mom."

"I won't," Kelly agreed. "But how long are you keeping it a secret? I mean, you're not going to hide them in a closet once they're born, right? And people will notice that they're not normal dogs or cats... won't they?"

Lashonda told Kelly about how risky these hybrid pregnancies were—every other prospective mother before her and Vienne had miscarried by this point. Then, the sisters talked together, speculating about the growing litter. They agreed that Kelly should fly out to meet the babies just as soon as they were born. However, Lashonda couldn't help whispering inside her head, "*if they're born.*"

Every day until the three month mark felt like a day of holding her breath.

~

LASHONDA WANTED to celebrate her three month appointment with Dr. Flockhart by spending a quiet evening at home with Topher afterward, but Vienne had other ideas. She found out when the appointment would be, talking to Lashonda one day, and immediately made reservations at a trendy, new restaurant for four. She and Rick wanted to help Lashonda and Topher celebrate. It wasn't what Lashonda had in mind, but she didn't want to disappoint her new friend.

The important part was that the appointment went well, and it did.

Vienne was so excited that she and Rick met Lashonda and Topher at their apartment early to help them get ready for the celebratory dinner. Lashonda wasn't showing yet, but Vienne's waist had started to thicken. Though, somehow, she managed to still have a different strappy, pink dress for every occasion.

"You should dress up, too," Vienne urged Lashonda.

"I only have one dress," Lashonda said.

Vienne insisted on seeing it, so they left Rick and Topher talking while Lashonda took Vienne into the bedroom to inspect the options.

After rifling through Lashonda's closet for several minutes, Vienne said, "You weren't lying. There is only one dress in here." Fortunately, the dress was an emerald, floor-length gown with a simple, rounded neckline. Vienne considered it eminently suitable for the restaurant they'd be going to, and, after some urging, Lashonda agreed to wear it.

The restaurant had a live band and a dance floor.

Lashonda barely felt like she had the energy to drag herself out of bed in the morning to lie on the couch these days, but

Vienne convinced her that she should take this last opportunity before her belly began to swell and bulge to get out on the dance floor and whirl around with her man.

Black cat and pug dog danced together; then the couples switched partners, and Lashonda danced with Vienne's ginger tom for a while. When they switched back, she leaned against Topher's broad chest, letting him support her weight while she rested against him.

"I'm so tired, all the time," she said.

"I know," Topher whispered, his face beside her ear. "But you're more than a third of the way through this, and when you're done, you'll get to hold your puppies and kittens."

"Puppies *and* kittens," she said, happily. "*Both*." Then her stomach turned icy. "Unless something goes wrong…"

"Nothing is going to go wrong," Topher said. "Look at Vienne."

Despite her thickened waistline, Vienne pirouetted lightly in Rick's arms. Her pink dress flared out as she twirled.

"She's a month ahead of you," Topher said. "And she's doing fine. You're doing even better. By this point, she'd lost one of her litter, and her litter was smaller to begin with. So, as long as she's okay, you have nothing to worry about."

Lashonda nodded, her head still mashed against Topher's chest as they swayed together to the music. She only had another four to five months to go—depending on whether hybrid litters had a gestation length closer to that for cats or for dogs. She chanted numbers in her mind, one through six, counting her babies, over and over in her head. She had the sense that she'd be doing that a lot for the next few months.

CHAPTER 11

Vienne went into seclusion after that night. She afforded Lashonda a standing invitation to visit her penthouse apartment in the Angelique District, especially if she brought take-out. However, Vienne didn't want to deal with the tabloids finding out she was pregnant, so she retired her signature pink, strappy dresses and only left her apartment on rare occasion, wearing a frumpy, tweed trench coat.

Several nights a week, Lashonda spent the evening at Rick and Vienne's, eating take-out and watching The Nightly Howl with them on their giant television.

Two more months passed. Lashonda and Vienne's friendship grew closer as each of their bellies grew larger. Lashonda submitted the paper she'd written about her synthesizer to the top engineering journal, *Otter Mechanical*, and Topher began preparing extra routines so that he could take a break from joke-writing after their litter was born.

Then, disaster struck.

Vienne went into labor early.

Rick called from the docks. Lashonda answered, and his image appeared on the vid-screen—his orange ears stood at half mast; his whiskers turned down; and, his eyes looked haggard. "I can't do this alone," he said. "I keep telling Vienne that everything is going to be okay, but it's not going to be okay."

Lashonda's chest tightened. "What happened?"

"Vienne's in labor. We've done everything we can to stop it, but the contractions keep coming." Rick looked away from the camera. Lashonda realized she could see Vienne in the background, huddled on a bench crying. Rick must have been using one of the payphones at the docks. "I called Dr. Flockhart, and she's sending a water taxi to get us and bring us over to the isle. Can you come?"

Lashonda glanced around the apartment, picturing what she'd need to grab if she were to run out now. Then, she realized, it was too late in the day to take a ferry, and the water taxis were too expensive for it to make sense to hire one on her own. "I don't think I could get to the docks fast enough, Rick, and there won't be another ferry until the morning."

Rick's half-mast ears fell to completely flat, and a strangled sound escaped his throat.

"You'll do okay," Lashonda said. "As soon as you get there, Nelly and Dr. Flockhart will take care of you."

They both knew that wasn't true. Nelly and Dr. Flockhart would take care of Vienne. Rick would sit, alone in a waiting room all night.

"I'll come on the first ferry," Lashonda said. "I promise. Me and Topher."

Rick nodded. His morose look spoke of death. Anyone who saw him would think he'd just seen someone die. And, for all they knew, he had. Unless the babies were moving, at any given moment, there was no one to know how they were doing without a heart monitor or an ultrasound.

"Take care of Vienne," Lashonda said. She felt like she was

babbling, saying anything that might distract and soothe Rick for a moment, because that was all she could do.

He ended the call, and Lashonda curled up on the end of her couch, wrapped herself around her own enigmatic belly, and counted the number of times she could feel her litter move while waiting for Topher to come home from The Nightly Howl. Her babies sounded like helicopters when Dr. Flockhart listened to them with the heart monitor, but they felt like butterflies or bubbles. Light and airy. She feared squeezing them too tight with her expectations and anticipation; they might disappear like a dream.

Lashonda awoke when she heard Topher come through the door, just enough to mumble incoherent words about Vienne, Rick, and the morning ferry as he picked her up and carried her to bed. He wasn't much taller than her, but he was built like a canine tank. Even with her growing weight, Topher could still easily lift his lady love. She sank back into her deep, dream-filled sleep.

Lashonda woke with the dawn, heart racing. She'd dreamed all night about traveling to the ferry. Over and over again, she'd taken the train through the subway tunnels, always arriving back at home and needing to get herself ready to travel to the ferry again. It was a relief to break out of the cycle. This time, in the true light of day, the train would take her to the ferry; the ferry would take her to Friedan Isle; and, she could spend the day supporting her friends.

Before she even got dressed, though, Lashonda found a message waiting for her—a simple text message from Rick that said, "Don't bother coming. We lost the litter."

Lashonda cried for Vienne. She cried for Rick. She cried for the lost Chihuahua-kittens. And she cried because her own litter of six would now be the first hybrids ever born, and that was too far fetched to believe. If dogs and cats had been meant to breed with each other, humans would have designed them that way to begin with.

The next month was a lonely one. Lashonda wasn't surprised that Vienne and Rick no longer answered her calls. She didn't blame them. However, it did leave her completely isolated. Lashonda decided to go into seclusion for the last months of her pregnancy like Vienne had. She spent her days watching science shows on one of the otter channels and, occasionally, talking to Kelly over a vid-call. Topher brought her food. She didn't even want to deal with the delivery dog from her favorite Szechwan restaurant.

Lashonda's appointments with Dr. Flockhart grew more frequent, and Dr. Flockhart grew more solicitous. Instead of asking a few cursory questions about her health and sending Lashonda on her way, Dr. Flockhart greeted Lashonda personally when she arrived for appointments, showed true concern for her health and *feelings*, and began urging Lashonda to consider moving to Friedan Isle for the remainder of her pregnancy.

"We could keep better track of your progress if you lived closer," Dr. Flockhart said during one of the ultrasounds.

The babies looked recognizably like little animals on the ultrasound screen now, but Lashonda couldn't tell whether they looked more like kittens or puppies. Watching them on the ultrasound screen, listening to the helicopter-beats of their hearts was the only time Lashonda felt safe. Yet, she didn't want to move to Friedan Isle, so she simply smiled, polite but cool, at Dr. Flockhart's suggestions.

"If you're worried about the cost, we'd be happy to have you stay here."

Lashonda frowned at the small, sterile, medical room around them.

"Not in the offices," Dr. Flockhart said. "Nelly and I have a spare room upstairs. You could stay with us there. We'd be happy to have you."

"Thank you," Lashonda said. "I'll think about it."

In the elevator, on their way out, Topher asked, "Will you really think about it?"

"No," she said. "You need to stay in the city for The Nightly Howl. And, whatever benefits there might be to staying closer to my doctor, there are more benefits for me staying close to you." Lashonda ran a paw affectionately over Topher's shoulder and down his chest. She felt too awkward and off-balance to hold his paw while they walked anymore, but she didn't think she could sleep at night without him snuggled beside her.

"I'll talk to Jeckie," Topher said. "Maybe I can take some time off from the show. I plan to after the babies are born anyway."

"What will you tell him?" Lashonda asked. The closer they got to the birth, the harder their secret became to keep.

"I don't know," Topher said. Neither of them knew what to expect when their secret got out, and it was hard to plan for the unknown.

NEWS SPLASHED ACROSS THE COUNTRY, from coast to coast, that the first hybrid litter had been born. Photos of the proud mama calico holding her curly-haired poodle-kittens graced the front page of every news site. The babies had perfect kitten faces and flowing, white poodle tresses. They were beautiful like angels; the world reviled them like devils.

Death threats. Rocks hurled through windows. Burning effigies. The calico and her teacup poodle husband were afraid to go home, and a guard was set up around their hospital. Churches organized marches and rallied against the abomination sheltered inside the hospital's walls. Other churches organized a defense—not because they believed hybridization was right, but because they believed violence, even against abominations, was wrong.

Lashonda devoured the articles with terror as they rolled in. Glued to her computer screen, she watched the horror story in West Kansas unfold until it came to its abrupt end.

A DNA test showed that the kittens were kittens. The calico's doctor had conned her, impregnating her with embryos fertilized by a Selkirk Rex—a rare breed of cat with curly, poodle-like fur. There wasn't a trace of canine DNA in them.

Death threats abated. A church group repaired the windows. A candlelight vigil was held around the calico woman's house to welcome her, her cuckolded poodle husband, and the Selkirk Rex kittens home.

The world breathed a sigh of relief. The species barrier between cats and dogs was safe. Only charlatans and con-artists would claim otherwise.

CHAPTER 12

Lashonda awoke in the dark of night with pain constricting her belly. It shot across her abdomen like lightning, leaving her shaken and unsure whether it would return.

Topher lay beside her on the bed, sound asleep and snoring softly. She didn't want to wake him.

Under the covers, Lashonda ran her paws over the fur of her distended belly. She wished the babies would move so she'd know they were okay. Instead, pain knocked the breath out of her. The contractions kept coming; they wouldn't let her sleep. She had no choice but to wake Topher.

She pushed his shoulder, rocking his body, and he snuffled awake. Still bleary, he asked, "What's going on?" She didn't answer right away, so he sat up, alarmed. "Are you okay?"

"Contractions," she said. She could barely drag the single word out of herself. She didn't want to acknowledge what was happening. That might make it real. "What happened to Vienne..." She wrapped her arms around herself. "What if it's happening to me?"

"You've already made it farther than her." Topher caressed Lashonda's shoulders. His rough paw pads stroked down her fluffing-out fur. "Your whole pregnancy has been different. But I can call Dr. Flockhart if you want."

Lashonda didn't want to bother Dr. Flockhart in the middle of the night for nothing. "It's too early," she said. "It has to be a false alarm." Her voice sounded unnaturally high and hysterical. She started shaking, and another contraction doubled her over. When the pain stopped, she whispered, "I need Dr. Flockhart."

Topher was already making the call.

THE WATER TAXI came for them at the docks, just like it must have come for Rick and Vienne. Moonlight spilled over the bay, and, when they got close enough, Friedan Isle glittered like a million diamonds above the water.

From inside the cabin of the water taxi, Lashonda watched the beauty of the night with eyes haunted by death. Every thought she had was about death. It lurked everywhere her mind turned: Vienne's litter, the threats against the alleged poodle-kittens, and now a pain that wracked her body so badly she didn't understand how it hadn't killed her. How could one body hurt so much and not die?

Josh, the yellow Labrador nurse, met the water taxi at Friedan Isle's dock. He was a large dog and easily swept Lashonda, pregnant belly and all, up in his arms. She heard the splashing water of the rivulet beside them as Josh carried her down the walkways, into the building, up the elevator, and finally into Dr. Flockhart's office.

Nelly and Dr. Flockhart met them in the front lobby and ushered Josh with Lashonda still in his arms into one of the operating rooms. He arranged her on a table while Nelly told her to hold still. She could hear Topher talking to Dr. Flockhart, but she couldn't hear what either of them was saying.

"Am I about to meet my babies?" she asked, her voice loud and uncertain.

Nelly and Josh both looked at Dr. Flockhart, but then they continued what they'd been doing without answering. Nelly continued setting up the ultrasound machine. Josh said, "This will pinch for a moment, but then you'll feel better." Lashonda felt a small, sharp pain in her back. It was nothing compared to the contractions.

Then a feeling of warmth flooded over her.

Dr. Flockhart stepped up to the table and stood over Lashonda. She pressed the heart monitor against Lashonda's belly, and the sound of tiny helicopters filled the room. The amorphous puppy-like shape of her babies appeared on the ultrasound screen, green and ghostly.

Topher grabbed one of Lashonda's paws and squeezed until her claws pierced his paw pads, but Lashonda didn't look at him. Her eyes were locked on Dr. Flockhart, trying to read any nuance of expression as those crystal blue canine eyes examined the ultrasound screen.

The longer Lashonda stared at Dr. Flockhart's mottled gray muzzle and tufted ears, putting all her hope and faith in this one Australian Shepherd, the more she began to believe that Dr. Flockhart must be the most beautiful, wonderful dog in the world. Dr. Flockhart would take care of her.

As the minutes passed, Lashonda's pain subsided. Her body stopped shaking.

Finally, Dr. Flockhart smiled, splitting her muzzle into a dazzling grin. "No," she said. "You're not going to meet your litter tonight. Disappointed?"

Lashonda's ears flicked and skewed in a confusion of emotions. "Yes?" she said. "I guess? I mean, they're not ready yet, are they?"

"No," Dr. Flockhart said. "They could use a few more weeks in there."

"But... Does that mean I have to do this again?" Lashonda's voice broke. "And more?"

Dr. Flockhart laughed, and Lashonda couldn't help feeling that any amusement at her suffering was inappropriate.

"Usually, you would, yes," Dr. Flockhart said. "But, in this case, I think a cesarean would be safer. So, no, you don't have to do that again."

"What if," Lashonda's voice shook as she spoke, "this happens again while I'm at home?"

Dr. Flockhart smiled sympathetically, but her voice held an iron-clad authority: "You're not going home. Not until after the babies are born."

Lashonda looked at Topher for support, but he gave her the same sympathetic smile. "I packed your bag before we left."

Lashonda tried to argue, but exhaustion overtook her. Half-dreaming, she felt the nurses, Dr. Flockhart and Topher lift and roll her onto a gurney. She floated down the hallway, hearing the squeaky wheels of the gurney beneath her. The sterile walls and harsh lighting of the medical offices gave way to natural dawn light from windows decorated with flowered curtains and gauzy sashes.

Paws grabbed her, lifting and rolling her again, out of the gurney. Plush white covers and sheets welcomed her, and she sank into their downy embrace.

DAYS AND NIGHTS blurred together as Lashonda lay in the downy folds of the bed in Dr. Flockhart and Nelly's guest room. At first, she watched the world change through the tiny pane of her laptop computer screen, balanced uncomfortably in front of her bulging belly.

Government committees met to discuss the banning of hybridization gene therapy. Panels of scientists argued about whether it was even possible. And Topher joked on The Nightly Howl, ridiculing the very idea of puppy-cats.

Then Nelly took her laptop away.

She couldn't really object. After all, her stress over the news about the Selkirk Rex kittens had almost thrown her into an early labor. Topher told her anything she wanted to know about the news when he visited anyway. Somehow, it was less upsetting that way, hearing it in her husband's voice.

The church-dogs who rallied in protest of hybridization looked less angry in her imagination than they must on the news reports, and Jeckie Danson's wry irony was less cutting.

In Dr. Flockhart's guest room with all her meals brought to her by Nelly, Lashonda felt safe and cut off from the rest of the world. The way the light filtered softly through the gauzy window dressings made her room feel like it was in a castle on a cloud, untouched by the turmoil in the world back on the mainland.

Thus, she didn't understand the rattling against her window when she heard it. She thought it must be rain or hail, but the light was bright enough that she didn't expect a storm. Lashonda got out of the bed and padded over to the window. She drew back the gauzy shade, wondering if the combination of sun and storm would fill the skyline of this golden city with a rainbow.

Blinding sunlight filled the room. Not a cloud marred the bright blue sky. Lashonda narrowed her eyes, confused, as she looked out at the glittering, golden buildings that filled her window's view.

She heard muffled sounds like a crowd of people, then rocks startled her as they slammed, rattling against the window pane. Lashonda ducked instinctively beneath the window's sill. When the rattling died down, she crept closer and peeked outside. This time she looked down.

Angry dogs and cats holding signs that read, "Hybrids Be

Damned!", "Kill the Abominations!", and other horrifying phrases, filled the walkways and several small boats moored in the rivulet below.

"Nelly?!" Lashonda cried out, her voice quavering. Her paws spread over her belly as if to protect the babies inside from the anger and violence below.

Instead of Nelly, Josh came. He put his paws on her shoulders and guided her away from the window. "Nelly's busy," he said.

"What's happening?" Lashonda asked as Josh sat her down on the bed. He drew the curtains shut again, flinching as the glass shattered behind them. The roar of the crowd grew louder without the glass muffling it. "Stay back from the window," he said. Then he started pulling clothes out of one of the dressers. When he found a baggy sweat suit, he threw it over to Lashonda. "Here, put this on." It looked like it would barely fit over her belly. Lashonda pulled the clothes on anyway.

"Here's the deal," Josh said. "Kevin's wife left him last week. This morning, he was on the news, railing about how mixed-species marriages are wrong, and he's done doing the devil's work."

Lashonda's green eyes widened. "Kevin told the news about Dr. Flockhart?"

"That's right," Josh said. "And now we need to get off of Friedan Isle." He held out a paw to help Lashonda up from the bed. "Can you swim?"

Down in the medical offices, they found Dr. Flockhart stuffing Nelly's shirt with towels until it bulged like she was pregnant. Dr. Flockhart pulled Nelly against her, embracing her hard—an Australian Shepherd hugging a pregnant black cat.

Dr. Flockhart turned to Josh and gave him a piercing stare with her hard blue eyes. "You take care of Nelly."

Josh's ears flopped as he nodded. Then, he and Nelly headed toward the front elevator.

Dr. Flockhart turned to Lashonda and said, "We'll give them five minutes. Then we're going down. I need you to trust me."

Lashonda swallowed. Her throat was dry. "Where's Topher?" she asked.

Dr. Flockhart reached out and took her paw. The tufts of fur were long between her paw pads. "Wherever he is, he'd want you safe. Come with me, and he'll catch up with you later."

Five minutes later, the elevator doors opened on a massive crowd, barking and yowling, but thankfully turned away from the building. Somewhere in that crowd, Josh shielded Nelly, the two of them fighting their way down the walkways.

Dr. Flockhart pulled Lashonda by the paw toward the rivulet. They didn't have a boat, and they couldn't waste time trying to hire one. Besides, the crowd would expect to find a pregnant cat keeping dry. So, whenever they figured out that Nelly wasn't her, Lashonda needed to be in the one place they wouldn't think to look for her—in the water.

At the edge of the rivulet, Lashonda froze, terrified. She'd never swum before. She'd always meant to try, some day, but she'd never planned to do it when she was large and clumsy, awkward with the bulk of a litter.

The water lapped against the ledge of the walkway with the ceaseless motion of ocean waves in miniature. It would wait for her forever, but the angry crowd behind her wouldn't. Lashonda drew a deep breath, knelt down, and with a helping paw from Dr. Flockhart lowered herself into the tepid water. Her skin crawled as its wet touch crept up her body.

When the waterline reached the middle of her bulging belly, Lashonda lost her balance and, thrashing in panic, lost hold of Dr. Flockhart's paw. She fell the rest of the way into the water, splashing inelegantly. Out of control, her paws flailed, and her head bobbed in and out of the rivulet. She gulped for air but gagged on saltwater.

Splashing and commotion beside her was followed by paws grabbing her shoulders and squeezing hard. "*Don't thrash.*"

Lashonda's eyes locked on the source of the words. Bobbing with her in the water, Dr. Flockhart held her tightly, her sure blue canine eyes instilling calm until Lashonda surrendered. Her body relaxed, and she found that the saltwater buoyed her up. She felt lighter floating in the ocean than she had on solid ground for months.

Above them on the walkway, the crowd continued to bark and howl, oblivious to the Australian Shepherd and pregnant black cat who'd joined all the otters slicing their way through the waters of the rivulet like cars careening down a freeway.

Unlike a river on land, the rivulets on Friedan Isle didn't have currents. They were shaped narrow like rivers but stood still like a lake. So, while brown-furred bodies raced by, Dr. Flockhart and Lashonda floated in place, only feet from the angry crowd that could notice them any minute.

Dr. Flockhart put her muzzle close to Lashonda's ear and shouted over the noise of the crowd, "I need you to swim with me." She let go of Lashonda's shoulders, and the two of them floated in the water, facing each other. "Good," she said. "Now, this way." Dr. Flockhart kicked with her feet and stroked with her front paws, smoothly pulling herself through the water toward the middle of the rivulet.

Lashonda tried to emulate her, but her paws felt useless clawing at the water. She didn't glide forward like Dr. Flockhart, merely drifted a little. She clawed harder in frustration, but her muscles didn't know the rhythm for swimming.

Dr. Flockhart made it to the middle of the rivulet, stopped, and looked back. Her head bobbed at the surface of the water, muzzle frowning. On the far side of the rivulet, behind her, the walkway was filled with more angry picketers, holding their condemnation-filled signs. They were all around, on both sides of the rivulet, and between all the buildings. Lashonda couldn't imagine swimming far enough to get away from them.

Dr. Flockhart put her head down and swam back to Lashonda. Putting her muzzle close to Lashonda's ear again, she said, "Hold onto my shoulder. I'll help pull you along." Dr. Flockhart was a medium-sized dog and stood a good head taller than Lashonda. Her shoulders felt broad and safe as Lashonda wrapped her paws around them. Then Dr. Flockhart began to kick and stroke, and Lashonda felt the water rush by as they surged forward.

Together they swam for what felt like hours in the rivulets of Friedan Isle, passing one golden skyscraper after another until the angry mobs thinned out. They swam deep into the city, away from the ferry docks.

When they finally climbed out of the water, dripping, onto a walkway, Lashonda didn't think her body had ever felt so weary before in her life. Every muscle ached. Even the muscles in her ears ached from being held flat, tight against her head for the entire duration of her swim.

"I don't think I want to be an otter anymore," she told Dr. Flockhart as she lay on the ground, shivering and dripping. She wanted to tell Topher, but he wasn't there.

Dr. Flockhart took her by the front paws and pulled her to her feet. "Come on," she said. "I've chartered a helicopter. There's a landing pad up ahead. That'll get us off the island."

Lashonda leaned heavily against Dr. Flockhart's arm. They walked two blocks, and then the buildings gave way to a flat tarmac with a single helicopter parked on it. Beyond the tarmac stretched the open ocean.

A large dog dressed in navy blue fatigues, wearing a shiny black helmet, climbed out of the helicopter and shouted across the tarmac, "Welcome to the smallest airport in the world! I hear that you ladies need to get out of here fast."

"That's right," Dr. Flockhart said.

"Well, I'm your dog!" He helped them into the back seat of the helicopter and gave them each helmets. "Put those on, we'll be on our way."

"Where are we going?" Lashonda asked.

"An airport on the mainland," Dr. Flockhart said, settling the helmet over her tufted ears. "After that, I don't know."

Lashonda pulled her own helmet over her ears, and the pilot dog helped her stretch the complicated seatbelt harness around her belly and snap the buckles. Then, he turned to the front console and began working the controls. The chopper blades roared to life. Their steady whirring sounded nothing like the tiny heartbeats inside Lashonda's belly.

Lashonda had trusted Dr. Flockhart to care for those tiny heartbeats. She assumed that Dr. Flockhart knew what she was doing. But as Lashonda looked at Dr. Flockhart's frowning muzzle, she realized that her plan truly didn't stretch farther than this moment.

"I miss Topher," Lashonda said.

Dr. Flockhart's blue eyes got a faraway look. "I hope Nelly is okay."

The helicopter lifted into the air, and Lashonda saw through the window as the glittering, golden city on the ocean shrank away beneath her. "We need somewhere safe," Lashonda said. She'd thought Friedan Isle was safe.

"We need to get away from all the political turmoil," Dr. Flockhart said.

"There weren't any otters in those crowds," Lashonda realized. Looking back toward the city, all she could see was an intricate golden jewel on the horizon, but she knew the streets must still be crowded with rioting cats and dogs.

"No," Dr. Flockhart said. "Otters can't afford to hate hybrids —their whole genetics are based on a hybridization of thirteen different species. They've been that way since humans first uplifted them." She leaned back in her seat and closed her eyes. "Studying otter biology on Deep Sky Anchor is where I came up with most of my ideas."

"You studied on Deep Sky Anchor?" Lashonda said. For so long, she'd wanted to go there. It would be far away from the political turmoil between the cats and dogs on Earth. "That's somewhere my litter would be safe."

Dr. Flockhart opened her eyes with a start. She gave Lashonda a piercing stare and said, "I'll call up my old advisor when we get to the airport. He might be sympathetic to our cause."

Empty blue passed beneath the helicopter, and the silvery skyline of Old York appeared on the horizon.

"Of course," Dr. Flockhart said, "Living on the space station is crazy expensive. We should probably come up with a backup plan."

Lashonda snorted. "You're worried about money?"

Dr. Flockhart's blue eyes narrowed. "All my equipment, everything I have is tied up in that lab on Friedan Isle. You don't think I get rich trying to break scientific ground, do you?"

"I'm sorry," Lashonda said. She couldn't stop herself from adding, "Though, you could if you wanted to."

"What do you mean?"

Lashonda's eyes widened. "You could charge Vienne anything you wanted to let her and Rick try to have a litter again. Name your price, I'm sure she'd pay it."

"Vienne Howard?" Dr. Flockhart asked blankly.

"Your patient," Lashonda said.

"I know." Dr. Flockhart sounded annoyed.

"Don't you know who she is?"

The pilot dog looked back from his seat up front. "I'm sorry, folks, but you don't know who Vienne Howard is? Pretty little Chihuahua, famous for being rich?"

"She is?" Dr. Flockhart asked.

"Damn," he said. "You really don't know about her." He shook his helmeted head and turned back to the controls.

"Don't you run extensive background checks on all your patients?" Lashonda asked.

"Kevin ran the background checks; I ran the genetic tests after couples passed them."

Lashonda could see the gears turning in Dr. Flockhart's head.

"I guess I'll give Vienne a call when we get to the airport, too."

"And I'll call Topher."

CHAPTER 13

The helicopter carried them to an airport on the mainland where Dr. Flockhart took control again. She arranged flights for herself and Lashonda to Mexico and from there to Guatemala. She called Vienne on an airport phone and bartered her services in exchange for full funding of new medical offices and a lab on Deep Sky Anchor. Then she called her graduate otter advisor, and he agreed to let her use his facilities on the space station until her own were set up—in return for a few pieces of new lab equipment.

Watching Dr. Flockhart make her calls, cool and collected, Lashonda felt safe and cared for again. Dr. Flockhart was a sheep dog, and Lashonda was her sheep. Though, she knew it was only temporary. Once her litter was born, she'd no longer be Dr. Flockhart's patient. Dr. Flockhart would have proven her point—she could genetically engineer a hybrid litter between a cat and a dog. Caring for that litter would be Lashonda's responsibility.

"What will we do once the litter is born?" Lashonda asked Topher over the airport phone. She wasn't sure that she'd want to come home. After everything she'd seen, she wasn't sure her litter would be safe on Earth. She hoped the space station would be different, but she knew they wouldn't be able to afford to stay there for long, not with Topher's job back on Earth and her unemployed.

Topher's expression was hard to read on the small, grainy phone-screen, but he said, "Just focus on staying safe and healthy for now. We'll figure the rest out later."

"I wish you could make it to the airport in time to fly with us," Lashonda said.

"Me too. Have a good flight, and I'll meet you at the space station." He gave her a cheesy grin. "Try not to have our litter without me."

Lashonda had no desire to give birth on an airplane or the space elevator. "I'll see what I can do."

Airplane seats are never especially comfortable, doubly so when carrying a full-term litter of six. Being a cat, Lashonda was never too large for an airplane seat, since they had to be large enough to accommodate large-breed dogs. However, the stiff cushions and weird angles felt like torture devices beneath her pregnant body. Lashonda twisted to one side and then the other, tilted her hips, squiggled and squirmed in every way to relieve the weight of her enormous belly pressing down on her spine. All the while, Dr. Flockhart sat stock-still in the seat beside her with headphones over her ears, watching otter news on the seatback vid-screen.

Lashonda tried to sleep. She mostly failed, instead drowsing in and out of consciousness while staring at the otter news anchors dressed in their sharp suits on Dr. Flockhart's vid-screen.

Several hours into the flight, Lashonda dreamed she saw Topher anchoring the news among the otters. Drifting closer to consciousness, she realized it wasn't entirely a dream: Topher was onscreen. The otter show was running a clip from The Nightly Howl. Lashonda switched on her own seatback vid-screen, flipped to the right channel, and put on the earphones to hear what he was saying.

"—can you imagine? Cats living on Europa? That's an ice planet, and cats like their sunlight."

Lashonda recognized the joke. It was comforting to hear her husband's voice, but she wondered what was so remarkable about this particular routine that an otter news station would show a clip from it. Then Jeckie Danson walked onscreen.

Lashonda could tell that Topher was discomposed by Jeckie's presence. It must not have been planned. Jeckie didn't say anything; he simply stood to the side of the screen watching. Topher soldiered on, saying, "The only thing chillier than a cat on an ice planet must be a Chihuahua without a sweater. By the way, Vienne, honey," Topher gave the camera a lecherous grin, "you left your sweater at my place last night, swing by to get it tonight. That is if Daddy Howard hasn't bought you a whole sweater factory to replace it by now."

Jeckie stepped forward. "You were with Vienne last night?"

"Uh, yeah," Topher said. He was doing his best to cover it, but he had no idea what was going on. Lashonda could tell.

"How does your *cat wife* feel about that?" Jeckie asked, his voice dripping with malice.

Jeckie had known about Lashonda all along, but they'd agreed she wouldn't be part of Topher's onscreen persona.

"I don't know what you're talking about," Topher said, keeping his face blank and his options open.

The two dogs—small pug and large, shaggy English Sheepdog—stared each other down. Finally, Topher gave Jeckie a big, jowly grin and said, "What can I do for you, Jeckie?"

Jeckie brushed his long white fur out of his eyes and said, "I have a joke I'd like to try out on you. What do you call a dog who makes fun of cats on the air but goes home to one he's knocked up with a litter of mongrel monstrosities?"

The question hung in the air between them. Finally, Topher pulled himself together enough to offer, "A player?"

"Try *fired*."

Lashonda wasn't sure what Jeckie expected, but he looked surprised when Topher shot back the answer, "It's a good try, Jeckie, but I think the punch line could use a little work."

The clip from The Nightly Howl ended, and the vid-screen cut back to a panel of news anchor otters, laughing and quoting bits from the scene they'd just shown. "Priceless!" one of them exclaimed, but Lashonda took off the earphones before he said any more. She couldn't handle any more right now.

Between worrying about the health of her litter, the terror of knowing her belly would soon be sliced open, and the danger of the rioting mobs who'd filled the walkways of Friedan Isle—she didn't have room inside her to worry about anything else. Even if that something else was Topher and how heartbroken he must be to lose his dream job... or wondering what they would do for money now.

Dr. Flockhart took off her earphones as well. "That didn't look fake," she said.

Lashonda shook her head.

"Bad time to lose his job, huh."

Lashonda nodded.

They sat in awkward silence, but Dr. Flockhart didn't put her earphones back on.

A flight attendant walked by offering packets of salted jerky and tuna crisps. Lashonda asked for one of each. Once the attendant passed on, Dr. Flockhart said, "I'm sure it won't take the sting out of the news you just got, but if either of you needs a job on Deep Sky Anchor, I'll need a replacement for Kevin."

"Thanks," Lashonda said.

For the rest of the flight and the flight after that, the otter show ran the clip of Topher losing his job approximately once an hour. Lashonda didn't listen to it again, but she got to watch her husband's face as he lost his dream job over and over. Then the otter news anchors laughed every time.

She realized, Topher must have already lost his job when she'd called him from the airport. He must have been too embarrassed to tell her over the phone, or he hadn't wanted to worry her. Either way, the fact that he'd kept it secret made him feel very distant from her. She tried to imagine him taking Kevin's job and working for Dr. Flockhart. It was such a step down from national television; she feared it would destroy him. Though, she supposed, at least they'd get to stay on the space station.

She'd traded his job, their home, and everything about their lives for the unborn babies in her belly. She hoped they were worth it.

LASHONDA WENT into labor on the ride up the space elevator. At first, she thought the pain across her belly was a reaction to the changing altitude or air pressure, maybe the gravity, but the contractions kept coming. Dr. Flockhart stayed beside her, whispering reassurances—*her contractions were still far apart; labor took hours to progress, and the elevator ride was only an hour longer; there would be plenty of time to make it to a proper operating room before Lashonda delivered the litter.*

As Lashonda whimpered in pain, arms wrapped around her belly, she couldn't help but feel that her babies could have waited a little longer. All this pain was unnecessary, since Dr. Flockhart still planned to give her a cesarean. Besides, she couldn't stand the furtive, confused glances from the other passengers on the elevator car. Business otters commuting to space and tourist dogs on vacation looked at her, wondering what was wrong with the fat black cat. Maybe some of them recognized her as Topher Brooke's *cat wife* about to give birth to *a litter of mongrel monstrosities*. That was worse.

Why couldn't they keep their eyes on the view? It was a stunning, panoramic of Earth shrinking away and the blue sky opening up to dark space around them—Lashonda couldn't properly appreciate it in her pain, but it sure as hell had to be a lot better than staring at her. Stupid tourists. Stupid otters. A growl built deep in her throat. She was angry at the tourists and otters and anyone she saw, but she was growling at the pain. If the pain had been outside her, where she could sink her claws into it, she would have kicked and bit and shredded it to ribbons. But it filled her insides, and there was nothing of it for her to fight. So, she growled instead.

Lashonda had always thought that her first visit to Deep Sky Anchor would be by Topher's side. Instead, Dr. Flockhart shepherded her, and she keenly felt Topher's absence. He should be with her. He was why she was here.

A sea otter nurse with a wheelchair met the elevator car as soon as it docked at Deep Sky Anchor. Before anyone else was allowed off, the sea otter nurse and Dr. Flockhart helped Lashonda into the chair and wheeled her away. Doubled over, oblivious to the wonders around her, Lashonda sobbed and growled as the sea otter nurse pushed her through the space station's hallways to a perfectly normal operating room. Except for all the otters dressed in scrubs, wearing surgical masks over their muzzles, she could have been on Earth, still in Old York.

She wished she were.

She missed Nelly and Josh. Most of all, she missed Topher. She'd dreamed of coming to the space station and seeing all the otters, but now in every otter's eyes, she saw laughter. She saw the news otters laughing at Topher after he lost his job.

On Earth, she was a monster. In space, she was a laughing stock. And, no matter where she was, she was in *pain*.

The surgical masked otters lifted her from the wheel chair,

stripped her clothes off her, and wrapped a hospital gown around her before lifting her onto an operating table.

"Lean forward," Dr. Flockhart said. Her muzzle was covered by a surgical mask now too, but her blue eyes looked the same. Lashonda trusted those eyes.

A needle pricked her back, just above her tail, and then Lashonda began shaking. Her body flushed with heat. The otters laid her down flat on the operating table, spread her arms wide, and attached tubes and needles to them with surgical tape. Unable to move her arms, Lashonda felt as though she were being crucified. She tried to twitch her tail, but the entire lower half of her body had turned to stone, immovable as well.

The pain stopped, and her growling subsided.

The otter nurses draped a curtain around Lashonda's torso, shielding her own lower body—and giant belly—from her sight. She couldn't see Dr. Flockhart, the one person in the room she trusted, anymore, but she heard her voice, commanding and directing the otter nurses, coolly in command like a herd dog should be.

Lashonda felt tugging at her belly, a strangely painless sensation. The tugging grew wider and larger until Lashonda could hardly believe none of the babies had been pulled out yet. Every moment, she expected to hear Dr. Flockhart say they'd all been born and were hidden behind the curtain now. Instead, she felt more tugging.

If Topher were with her, he could look behind the curtain and tell her if their litter were okay, but Lashonda couldn't ask any of these otters she didn't know. She didn't know them; she didn't trust them. She couldn't ask Dr. Flockhart; she didn't want to disturb her concentration. Any hope her babies had of being born alive depended on Dr. Flockhart.

"Well, hello there," Dr. Flockhart said.

A tiny black-furred pug face, eyes tight-shut, appeared

above the curtain, held up in Dr. Flockhart's paws. Lashonda wanted to reach for her kitten—puppy?—but her arms were pinned. An otter took the baby and carried it to the far side of the room.

Lashonda's ears twitched and flicked in a complicated dance on her head, straining to hear any sound from the infant. She watched desperately, wishing she could move closer, as the otter placed the wet black-furred bundle on a scale, wiped it with towels, and wrapped it in a small blanket. Finally, its muzzle opened in a cry, and Lashonda heard a trilling squeal unlike any sound she'd heard before. Her arms ached with the desire to reach out and hold it.

The tugging continued at her belly, and another tiny face was held up for her inspection—this babe had a black muzzle like the first, but, when the otter nurse took it, Lashonda saw that its body was tawny like Topher's. She wished he were here to see it.

One after another her babes were taken from her and swaddled in blankets by the otter nurses. Like her and Topher, each of them had a black face and ears. Three of them had tawny bodies.

Even after all six babes had been removed, the tugging continued while Dr. Flockhart sewed her back up. Finally, the first babe was brought to her and nestled beside her in the crook of her arm. She still couldn't move, but she could feel the warmth of the small bundle against her fur.

A purr rippled in her throat, vibrating stronger and stronger until Lashonda felt her entire body buzzing with the overflowing purr.

The otters undid the restraints that held her arms in place, and she immediately reached for the babe beside her. Tubing trailed after her arms, but she didn't care.

An otter nurse brought her a second babe, then a third. Once she had five babes piled in her arms, warm against her body, Lashonda felt as if she were holding an entire world. A whole lifetime's worth of family, love, and happiness filled her arms. She cried from happiness, tears mixing with purrs.

"These three are girls," an otter nurse said, pointing to two tawny-bodied babes and one all black one. "These two are boys." Both boys were all black; one with a pug face like his father, the other with a more delicate, feline muzzle but flopped over, canine ears.

"Where's the sixth?" Lashonda asked, craning her neck to see past the plethora of otter nurses filling the room. "Where did it go? I saw it before..."

Lashonda looked at the otter nurse in front of her, and, although his muzzle was covered with a surgical mask, the distress was clear in his eyes. Lashonda knew what he was going to say, and her stomach turned cold. Her purrs died away.

"I'm sorry," the nurse said. "The sixth one didn't make it."

Lashonda understood now how Vienne had mourned for the one she'd lost instead of celebrating the two who remained. Her arms were full of impossible, amazing, life-filled babes, trilling and mewling for her attention, but her heart broke for the one babe she didn't hold.

A tiny rumbling in her arms drew Lashonda's attention. She looked at the flat pug-face of one the three girls—with her tawny body and flopped ears, she looked more like Topher than any of the others—but *she was purring*. Lashonda laughed, and the sound startled the babes in her arms. The boy babe with the delicate, feline muzzle opened his eyes, and although the color was lighter than Topher's, they were clearly a dog's eyes.

Lashonda squeezed her armful of babes against her, and the purr rekindled in her throat. Exhausted, they all fell asleep together, a pile of purrs and cuddles.

CHAPTER 14

Throughout the night and the next day, otter nurses checked on Lashonda and her bundle of puppy-kittens every hour or so, helping care for the babes and checking everyone's vitals. The feeling slowly and prickly returned to Lashonda's legs, but the nurses urged her to stay in bed and let them do anything she needed done anyway.

Time passed in a strange twilight way, defined more by the waking and sleeping patterns of the babes than by the perpetually dim lights in their room. Sleep slipped over Lashonda, and contentment filled her. She awoke when tiny muzzles nuzzled her wanting to nurse or when the weight of a tiny body left her side, lifted away by otter paws come to change and bathe the babes.

Occasionally, an otter nurse would stay and chat awhile. One of them told her that his wife had recently had a litter of three. They agreed to get their litters together for a play date when Lashonda was all recovered and the babes were old enough to play.

Finally, Lashonda awoke to a familiar presence in her room. "Topher," she said through a voice thick with sleep. "You made it."

Topher sat in a chair beside her bed, rocking and holding one of the babes—an all black girl with feline features except for flopped puppy ears—in his paws. "They're beautiful, Lashy," he said. The babe squeaked at Topher and gazed up at him with slitted, feline eyes. "Congratulations. You've changed the world."

The species barrier between cats and dogs had fallen. "Dr. Flockhart changed the world," Lashonda said. "I was just along for the ride."

Topher grinned. "How many dogs does it take to change the world?" He didn't wait for Lashonda to answer. "Five, but they're only half dog."

Lashonda laughed, happy to have Topher with her again. Wherever he was, that was her home.

They sat in silence together, listening to their babes breathe and purr. Topher took a second babe from her—this one tawny furred with a delicate feline muzzle. Lashonda thought she could almost pass for a big-boned Siamese.

"I'm calling that one Twila," Lashonda said.

Topher balanced Twila in one arm and the all black girl in the other. "What about this one?"

"I thought we could call her Nell. For Nelly."

"I like that," Topher said. "Nelly was very brave taking your place on Friedan Isle."

"Did you hear what happened to her?" Lashonda asked. "I hope she made it out okay."

"We were on the same ride up the space elevator. She seemed a little shaken up, but not hurt," Topher said. "What about the boys? Which one's Garret and which is Marshall?"

"You pick," Lashonda said.

"Okay..." He leaned forward to look at the three babe's arranged around Lashonda on her hospital bed—two black-furred boys and a tawny-furred girl. "Let's call the one with the flat muzzle Marshall. And, if you don't mind, I'd like to name the last girl for my grandmother—Dahlia."

"She does look the most like your family," Lashonda said. "Okay."

Topher played tenderly with Twila's tiny, tawny-furred paw. He pressed down on her pawpads, and needle-fine claws extended. "What do you know," he said. "Retractable claws." He shook his head in wonder. "My mother is going to go out of her mind when she holds her very own grandkittens in her arms." He looked up at Lashonda. "You don't mind if I invite her to visit, do you?"

"Can it wait a few weeks?" Lashonda asked, feeling very tired. "Until we're settled?"

"Oh, of course," he said. "Though, I hope you don't mind— Kelly's already on her way."

Lashonda loved the idea of seeing her sister. "That's fine," she said.

Lashonda watched Topher stare lovingly at his very own puppy-kittens, too lost in gazing at them to notice her gazing at him. "Are you happy?" Lashonda asked.

"Very," he said.

"I'm sorry you lost your job."

Topher laughed and smiled as if his job meant nothing to him now that he was a father, but Lashonda knew better. He would miss the spotlight. He was a comedian, and he needed to perform.

"I've been thinking about it," she said, "And I think you should stay home with the kittens. I mean, puppies." She looked at the three babes still in her arms. "Whatever they are. You should stay home with them and keep working on your routines until you can get another gig." She drew a deep breath and tried not to feel like she was throwing her own career away. "Dr. Flockhart offered me Kevin's job. It's not science, but it'll pay for us to stay here on the space station. It'll be safer for us here."

"It will be safer," Topher said. "That's why I packed up all our stuff before I left and asked Kelly to help me find an apartment when she gets here. But you don't have to work for Dr. Flockhart. I have a job."

His grin made Lashonda's heart beat with anticipation. "What do you mean?"

"When Jeckie fired me on the air, it made such a big splash that the Orbital Broadcasting Company was all over it."

Lashonda frowned. "Yes, I saw the otter news anchors laughing at you over and over again on the flight here."

"Why are you frowning?" Topher said. "I'm a comedian. I live to be laughed at."

"But not... I mean..." Lashonda sputtered.

Topher stopped her with a paw on her shoulder. "I've been offered my own show on the OBC," he said. "The Brooke Bark. It'll film right here on Deep Sky Anchor."

Lashonda closed her eyes and relaxed, really relaxed for the first time in months. She didn't have to take her litter home to the rioting mobs in Old York. She didn't have to take a job as a secretary for Dr. Flockhart. And she hadn't ruined Topher's career.

"Now if only I could get a job at an engineering lab up here, everything would be perfect," she said.

"I can't make any promises on that count," Topher said. "But I made sure to pack up all the pieces of that synthesizer machine you left lying around our apartment to have shipped here, and someone at Otter Mechanical called to say they'd like to talk to you about the article you sent them. So, maybe?"

Otter Mechanical was unlikely to offer Lashonda a job, but they might accept her article. It would be a while before she had time to give her full attention to engineering again anyway.

She rested her forehead lightly against the black pug-face of her first-born boy and felt her purr resonate with his.

"What's it like out there?" she asked. "On the space station. I haven't seen any of it yet. I was already in labor when we got here."

"You're going to love it!" Topher said. "Sometimes you can see the moon hanging in the sky from one side, larger than you've ever seen it before, while the Earth fills the sky on the other side of you. And, at night, Earth glitters with rivers of city lights like a planet filled with stars of its own."

Lashonda's whiskers lifted in a smile. "I can't wait to see it. When our litter's a little older, we can finally take that trip to Moonville Funpark together."

"That'll be great," Topher said. He was quiet for a moment, then he added cautiously, "I have to warn you though—you're going to have to learn how to swim. There's a lot of water out there."

"On a space station?" Lashonda asked.

"An *otter* space station," Topher said. "You know how the streets were rivers on Friedan Isle? It's not that different here."

Lashonda remembered swimming through the rivulets of Friedan Isle, weighted down by her bellyful of puppy-kittens, hiding from the rage of rioting church dogs. It would be much nicer teaching her litter how to swim, watching them splash and play, surrounded by accepting otters on Deep Sky Anchor.

"That's okay," Lashonda said. "I always kind of wanted to be an otter." Besides, as the mother of a litter that wasn't quite puppies or quite kittens, she didn't feel entirely like a cat anymore. But she did feel whole.

ABOUT THE AUTHOR

Mary E. Lowd is a prolific science-fiction and furry writer in Oregon. She's had more than 200 short stories and a dozen novels published, always with more on the way. Her work has won three Ursa Major Awards, ten Leo Literary Awards, and four Cóyotl Awards. She edited FurPlanet's ROAR anthology series for five years, and she is now the editor and founder of the furry e-zine *Zooscape*. She lives in a crashed spaceship, disguised as a house and hidden behind a rose garden, with an extensive menagerie of animals, some real and some imaginary.

For more information:
marylowd.com

To read Mary's short stories:
deepskyanchor.com

ALSO BY MARY E. LOWD

Otters In Space

Otters In Space

Otters In Space 2: Jupiter, Deadly

Otters In Space 3: Octopus Ascending

Otters In Space 4: First Moustronaut

Otters In Space Spinoffs

In a Dog's World

When A Cat Loves A Dog

Jove Deadly's Lunar Detective Agency (with Garrett Marco)

The Entangled Universe

Entanglement Bound

The Entropy Fountain

Starwhal in Flight

Entangled Universe Spinoffs

You're Cordially Invited to Crossroads Station

Welcome to Wespirtech

Beyond Wespirtech

Brunch at the All Alien Cafe

Xeno-Spectre

Hell Moon

The Ancient Egg

The Celestial Fragments (A Labyrinth of Souls Trilogy)

The Snake's Song

The Bee's Waltz

The Otter's Wings

Tri-Galactic Trek

Nexus Nine

Commander Annie and Other Adventures

The Necromouser and Other Magical Cats

The Opposite of Memory

Queen Hazel and Beloved Beverly

Some Words Burn Brightly: An Illuminated Collection of Poetry

Furry Fiction Is Everywhere (with Ian Madison Keller)

www.ingramcontent.com/pod-product-compliance
Lightning Source LLC
Chambersburg PA
CBHW061345160726
47995CB00001B/176